Skin Deep

Streetwise Jo a... ...
unlikely friendship as newcomers in a sleepy
seaside town. When police in search of drugs
raid Jo's houseboat home, she and Jaz decide
to do their own detective work—following
up rumours of smugglers nearby. They
discover that you can't always judge by
appearances, and what starts as fun soon leads
into danger.

This is journalist Hilary Brand's first novel.
She originally trained as a photographer and
her writing experience includes working on a
national newspaper and adapting children's
books for radio. She lives in South London
with her husband, two teenage sons, three
lodgers and a cat.

Skin Deep

Hilary Brand

A LION BOOK

Copyright © 1994 Hilary Brand

The author asserts the moral right
to be identified as the author of this work

Published by
Lion Publishing plc
Sandy Lane West, Oxford, England
ISBN 0 7459 2881 1
Albatross Books Pty Ltd
PO Box 320, Sutherland, NSW 2232, Australia
ISBN 0 7324 0835 0

First edition 1994

A catalogue record for this book is available
from the British Library

Printed and bound in Great Britain
by Cox & Wyman Ltd, Reading

Contents

1

Across the Bridge

Jo woke with a start to find her bedroom rocking gently. 'Oh, no!' she groaned. Not that she was scared. It wasn't the beginning of a natural disaster, just the dawning realization that she was late for school again.

The rocking movement meant that it was high tide. Jo, who had developed a boat-dweller's feel for the rhythms of the water, could sense even through her dreams that it spelt trouble. She pulled herself up to look out of the porthole. Sure enough, *Trade Winds*, which normally sat slightly askew on the muddy river bed, had been lifted up by the gently lapping water.

She looked across the river to the church tower, rising above the little town. If she screwed up her eyes, she could just make out the clock face. It was ten to nine.

The dream (a games lesson where Jo was thrashing Miss Davies with a giant rubber hockey stick, and ignoring her pleas for mercy) faded into the reality of another bad day at school. Not that being late was unusual for Jodi Katherine Thomas. In fact, being on time was the exception.

She threw on her uniform and went into the kitchen. The 'galley', Mum called it. A milk carton stood on the table. Jo sniffed it and decided against cereal. One slice of bread and a crust—Jo decided she didn't have time for toast anyway. A rummage in the cupboard produced a packet of crisps and an oaty crunch bar.

'Bye Mum,' said Jo to the lump under the bedclothes, as she passed the bedroom door. Being artistic, Mum worked 'when the creative urge took her'. It never took her before eleven in the morning, but occasionally after midnight. Last night had been one of those nights.

Jo pounded over the wobbly gangplank, grabbed her bike and cycled madly up the river path. The church clock chimed in the distance.

She swung left onto the long footbridge, ignoring the 'No Cycling' signs as usual, and narrowly avoided a woman with a pushchair, who stopped and shouted after her.

'Never mind, I'll get yer next time,' muttered Jo, pedalling furiously. It was going to be one of those days.

'Oh Mum,' wailed Jasmine Walcott as she surveyed herself in the mirror, 'I can't possibly wear this.'

'It's all right, it shows off your figure.' This remark from Alex, aged ten, was not as kind as it sounded. A 'figure' was something that Jasmine, aged thirteen, had not yet developed to her satisfaction. Jasmine walloped him one, in sisterly fashion, and his returning kick just missed Mum, on the way in with the toast.

'It's not that bad, sweetheart,' said Mum, wiping up the goo that baby Clifford called breakfast. 'Anyway, it was very kind of Mrs Trevinnick to give you those things of Myrtle's. I don't know how we'd have afforded it otherwise.'

Mum was right. What with moving house, money was a bit tight and uniform was expensive—especially when you considered how boring it was. Most of Myrtle Trevinnick's cast-offs weren't too awful. Except this cardigan. Jasmine took it off and stuffed it in her bag. 'I don't really need to wear it, it's quite warm.'

'The toast's getting cold,' said Mum. 'Sit yourself down. Nerves are always worse on an empty stomach.'

'I'm not nervous,' said Jasmine, checking her dinner money and games kit for the third time.

'She's not nervous, not my girl,' said Dad, looking up from opening the post. 'Why do people keep sending begging letters? They think that just because you're a Reverend you've got money to give away.'

'They don't know much about us then,' said Mum. Dad was the new pastor of Harbour Street Chapel. He had been in computers before he had 'felt the call', as he put it, 'to the Lord's work'. He had worked his way through Bible College, assisted at a big church in Birmingham for a couple of years, and now they had arrived here, to bring the gospel to this sleepy Sussex town, which was blithely unaware that it needed it.

Well, Dad would wake them all up, thought Jasmine. Though if last Sunday, his first, had been anything to go by, the people of Shoreham weren't quite ready for his natural enthusiasm. They did say a few 'Amen's and 'Praise the Lord's in the right places, but they didn't sound very keen. And when Dad had told them to turn to the person next to them, give them a big hug and tell them God loved them, he had been met by looks as

9

stony as Shoreham beach. It didn't bother Dad, though. Nothing did. He just went and gave the stoniest person a hug.

Jasmine sighed, and wished she was as unfazed as Dad. She also wished today wasn't Monday. She went through life going hot and cold with fear and embarrassment most of the time anyway. And today was the first day in a new school, in the middle of the term, in the middle of the second year, in the middle of this Sussex backwater where hers would probably be the only black face.

'Shouldn't you be going?' said Dad, interrupting the rising wave of panic inside her skull.

'No, I don't have to be there till nine,' said Jasmine, glancing at the clock. Its long hand was almost at the vertical.

An immediate panic is always better than fear of the unknown. Jasmine, calmer with a real crisis to face, gulped her tea, gave Dad a marmaladey kiss, grabbed her bag and set off at a run.

'Have a good day. We'll pray for you, sweetheart,' called Mum from the kitchen, and Jasmine knew they would. There and then round the table, with baby Clifford still playing aeroplanes. Talking to God came naturally to the Walcotts. Jasmine sometimes found it intimidating, but today it was a comfort.

Jo hurtled through the school gates, slammed her bike in the shed... and then strolled casually into school. She wasn't going to let anyone see she was rattled. Anyway there was no one about—except a black girl she'd never seen before, and she was looking far more worried herself.

Jasmine was feeling wretched. It was only ten minutes' walk from home to school, but she had managed to take a wrong turn and it had ended up more like twenty. By the time she'd arrived, the corridors were deserted and she couldn't find anyone to ask. She had wandered off towards the lockers in desperate search of inspiration, when this girl, an answered prayer, came along.

'Oi you, that's my locker!' Jasmine jumped. 'You new round 'ere?' said Jo, asking the obvious. Jasmine nodded nervously. 'You could use that one, it's Dozy Watkins' and he only comes in if there's an R in the month. What form're you in?'

'Mr Bernard—8BD, I think.'

'Oh dear, not Bernie, he's a right pain if you're late. And no one knows that better than me.'

At least that's what Jasmine thought she heard the girl say. It somehow gave her courage. Perhaps this toughie wasn't as confident as she seemed.

'You couldn't tell me where to go, could you?' asked Jasmine in a burst of bravery.

'Yeah, sure,' said the cocky girl, and Jasmine wondered if she knew that she was wearing her cardigan inside out.

Safely delivered to 8BD and Mr Bernard, who wasn't a pain at all, but quite nice, Jasmine's day began to improve.

So did Jo's. She had gained a cast-iron excuse for lateness. 'I met this new kid in the corridor and I was showing her where to go.'

'Very laudable, Jodi,' said Mrs Tomkins wearily. What she thought was, 'Well—at least it's original.' Jodi had an irritating habit of telling the truth just when you didn't expect it, and the gleam in her eye made Mrs Tomkins pass on to the eating habits of the Tudors without a murmur.

At round about half past three, every school breathes a huge collective sigh of relief, and today Jasmine was very much part of it. No one enjoys their first day at a new school, but it could have been worse, thought Jasmine as she joined the flow out of the gates. She hadn't made any friends, and people had stared at her rather a lot, but no one had been nasty.

She saw that girl ahead of her, the guardian angel, and thought about going to say thank you, but the girl launched herself into a crowd of others. 'She must have lots of mates already,' thought Jasmine.

'Hey,' said Jo. 'Anyone coming down the beach?' The conversation continued around her. She tried again. 'Sarah, Lizzie, wanna come over to the beach?'

They looked uneasily at each other. One girl appointed herself spokesperson. 'Not with you, Jodi Thomas.'

'Suppose you thought that was clever, getting us a detention.'

Jo couldn't resist a smirk. 'Mrs Morton winds up real easy, don't she? It was only ketchup.'

Nobody else laughed. 'Anyway, we're going down the rec.'

Jo followed the direction of their eyes to the other side of the road, where Tony Maggs and his mates were eyeing them discreetly.

'Oh, yuk.' That was all Jo had to say on the subject. She suddenly found something important to fiddle with on her bike, and stopped. They could go where they liked——she had other things to do anyway.

'Excuse me,' said a voice behind her. 'Thank you for showing me where to go this morning.'

'How goes it, then? D'ya like our school?'

'It's all right.'

'I've just thought. You're black.'

'What's wrong with that?' Jasmine's timidity was blown away in a burst of defensiveness.

'Nothin'——keep yer hair on. It's just unusual round here. I never thought about it before.'

'You must be the only one,' said Jasmine, an explosion of feelings tumbling out. 'Everyone else has been staring at me all day.'

'Yeah, well, they would. Bit thin on the ethnics round here. Nice place though, innit?'

'Mmm,' said Jasmine, still a bit doubtful.

'I'm from New Cross, see, in London. That's why I didn't notice. Bin here nearly a year now.'

'What's it like? Are people friendly?'

'They're OK.' Jo's voice said the opposite to her words, thinking of Sarah and Lizzie's traitorous defection. She tried to be more convincing. 'No, really, they're not bad. Bit snobby, some of them. Y'know—— "Daddy's just bought me another new pony"——that sort of thing.'

Jasmine didn't really know that sort of thing.

'So where you from, then?'

Jasmine sighed. Sometimes she wondered that herself. 'I was born in Swansea, that's Wales . . .'

'Welsh——oh well, you really are an ethnic minority then!'

' . . . but Dad's from Guyana and Mum's from Ghana.'

13

'Aren't they the same place?'

'Different continents.'

'Oh, yeah, right. So why'd you come 'ere from Wales?'

'I didn't. After Wales we went to Norwich, then Oxford, then Birmingham, now here.'

'Is your Dad on the run or something?'

Jasmine groaned inwardly again. Here came the next explanation. Nobody understood what the pastor of an Elim Chapel was.

'You mean he's a vicar?' said Jo.

'Well, sort of.' It was the nearest most people got.

They were walking through the churchyard. It was the short cut that everyone took to the High Street. The church door was open, and a smell—the smell of old churches—came out. It was musty, peaceful, unchanging. Jasmine's Birmingham church hadn't been like that. It was new, loud and chaotic. Jasmine sometimes wondered which sort God preferred. She wasn't sure, herself.

'What's your name, anyway?' the girl interrupted Jasmine's churchy musings. This was another question she hated.

'Bit pretty-pretty, innit? I'll call you Jaz.'

'What's your name, then?'

'Jodi Thomas.'

'Jo—that's nice. What does the D stand for?'

Jo changed the subject. A naff name like Jodi was best disguised. 'Ta-ra, I go off here.'

They had come to where the High Street turned abruptly as it met the river. Only the long footbridge carried on.

'Do you live on the beach then?'

14

It wasn't as silly a question as it sounded. The narrow spur of land on the other side of the bridge was universally known as the Beach. Bordered by the river on one side and the sea on the other, it had once been nothing but a barren shingly strip with a few ramshackle wooden cabins. Now it had been tamed: tarmacked and turfed and liberally spread with brick-built bungalows and holiday homes. Along the riverside were moored a row of dilapidated houseboats, a last reminder of its less respectable past.

'Well, sort of, I live on the river.' Jo said it with some pride. 'Wanna come and see?'

Jasmine was impressed. But she thought of Clifford's sticky cuddles, and of Mum and Dad and Alex wondering how she'd got on: 'No, I'd better get back now . . . But,' she added quickly, 'I'll come tomorrow.'

'OK, it's a deal. Meet yer after school tomorrow.' And Jo leapt on her bike to cycle across the footbridge.

The bike clanked as it always did on the middle of the bridge. The centre section had been designed to swing aside and let big boats further up the river. But no big boats came now. The river had silted up to a narrow channel at all but the highest tides, and the swing-bridge was rusted solid.

On one side, where the river widened to meet the sea, there were still cargo ships. Down there were the docks, the yards loading gravel and cement and the tiny lighthouse perched on the harbour mouth. On the other side, beyond the road bridge, it narrowed to a trickle, snaking between marshy fields dotted with sheep, until the Downs rose up and hid it from sight.

When the bike clunked off the metal and onto the

concrete, Jo looked up to see the familiar black and purple vision that was her sister. Abby was elfin pretty and outrageous. She was studying art and living in a flat in Brighton. 'She's brilliant, my sister is,' Jo would always say. Because that's what people always said about Abby.

'Wotcha sis!' Jo did her best wheelie and crashed into the wall.

Abby jumped. 'Oh ... hi.'

'Been to Mum's?'

'Yeah.' Abby's eyes kept darting back.

'Did she lend you any?' It was a standing joke that Abby only came home when she was broke.

'No, no. Well, I didn't go home.'

'You just said you did.'

'Look, it doesn't matter.' Abby's fierceness took Jo by surprise.

'OK, OK, don't get your knickers in a twist.'

It was almost as if Abby noticed her sister for the first time. 'Sorry kid ... You haven't got a fiver, have you?'

Jo's expression said, 'You must be joking.'

'All right, no sweat. Look, I gotta go. I'm having a party—Saturday week, why don't you come?' she called back as she hurried towards the town.

'Because Mum thinks I'm too young to follow in your wicked ways.' Jo called after her. Abby's wicked ways looked all right to Jo. But today ...

She could have sworn Abby's hands were shaking.

Off the bridge, turn right and five minutes along the river path stood *Trade Winds*, lopsided once more in the glistening mud. It was bordered by *Rimini*, which in a previous life fired torpedoes in the Mediterranean,

16

and *Gone Fishin'*, which in a moment of glory once chased a German sub in a Norwegian fiord. *Trade Winds* had also seen the heat of battle, landing British troops on French beaches to push back the enemy, but it had long since been laid to rest to end its days as a 'desirable river residence'.

There were dozens of houseboats along this stretch of river. They'd been there as long as anyone could remember, as scruffy and colourful as their owners. Some of those owners stood about now—a surprising number of them. There was a buzz of gossip, an air of something not quite at ease. Puzzled, Jo noticed a posse of policemen retreating to their squad cars, parked on the distant road.

Jo threw down her bike and thumped across the planks that served as a front path. Past the pansies, planted in an old car tyre, that did for a garden. She ducked her head to enter the doorway.

'Hi Mum . . . Mum? . . . What? . . .'

Jo stopped short. *Trade Winds* would never win any gracious living awards; it was always a bit of a mess . . . but this . . .

Everything was turned over—cupboards, drawers, cushions, books—as if an angry whirlwind had just run its course. Even Mum's paints lay squeezed out and discarded. Photos of a holiday in Provence (happier days when Dad was around, Abby in her first bikini, Jo chubby and embarrassingly naked) were tipped from their envelope on to the floor.

'Mum!' Jo panicked, expecting to see a trail of blood across the floor.

'Nice mess they made, didn't they?' Mum was at the kitchen table, reaching for a bottle.

'Mum, you haven't been drinking, have you?' It had been known, in the days before Dad left and there was a lot of shouting behind closed doors.

'I'm steadying my nerves.' Mum poured a glass. 'I'm entitled to after such insulting behaviour.'

'Who . . .? What happened?'

'Police—flat-footed pigs.'

'The cops, did they come here? What'd they do this for?'

'They had reason to believe we might be concealing illegal substances. They had a warrant to search the premises.'

'Illegal substances?'

'Drugs.'

'Coo, how exciting.'

'I'm glad you think so. As far as I'm concerned it's a gross indignity and I'm going to write a letter of complaint immediately.'

'But why here? They didn't find any, did they?'

'Of course not. They said they had a tip-off. According to them, someone's dealing drugs round here. They even think there might be smuggling involved.'

'Smugglers!'

'Though why they picked on us . . .'

'I wonder if they caught them.'

'It's the Greenpeace demo, that's what it is. Once you're on their computer, you're a troublemaker for ever.'

'Mum, you've never done drugs, have you?'

'Certainly not. All I've ever done is protest about the destruction of the planet. Pointing out the truth's a crime in some people's eyes. I'll write to my MP. It's time someone took a stand against police oppression.'

'Wouldn't they clear up the mess?'

'They offered,' Mum admitted grudgingly. 'But I made them get out as soon as possible. I'll claim damages.'

'Did they break anything?'

'That isn't the point. They might have done. Bursting into innocent people's homes!'

Mum's angry flow dried up and she leaned wearily on the table. 'I sometimes wonder about your sister, though.'

'Abby? Why?'

'Oh, she can't do anything wrong in your eyes, can she?'

Jo was about to retort, but noticed Mum's eyes were glistening as she knocked back her drink. She looked suddenly tired and scared.

'Never mind, Mum. This place needed a good sort out.'

Mum smiled wanly. 'Well, if you want any tea, you'd better help me start tidying.'

2

Young Detectives

'Smugglers? Wow——that's amazing.' Jasmine's breath-
less astonishment was gratifying. 'Wonder if they
caught them.'

'Nah, they didn't. They raided two boats and one
house, but they didn't find anything.' At least, that was
what neighbourhood gossip was saying, backed by
information from someone's brother-in-law's friend in
the Force.

Jasmine and Jo had met at the school gate the next
day. Jaz was now riding pillion on Jo's bike as they
crossed the bridge, and the conversation was shouted
against the wind.

'So the villains are still at large. You haven't seen
anything suspicious, have you?'

'Nah, not really. They're a funny lot round us. You
have to be pretty peculiar to live on a boat that doesn't
go anywhere.'

'I think it's a brilliant place to live.' Jaz was easily
impressed. Jo took on the role of guide—the Beach
was *her* patch.

They arrived at *Trade Winds*—tidy now. And Mum,
calmer today and behaving more like anybody else's

mother, served up a respectable cup of tea and some ginger cake, and related all over again exactly what had happened.

After tea, Jo took Jaz to explore the beach. They crossed over the green with its empty swings and windblown litter, past the retirement bungalows, tidy with garden gnomes and geraniums, and the weather-beaten holiday homes, buckets and spades lying abandoned in their porches.

And then the sea. The tide was out, distant beyond the tarred and grubby pebbles and the immaculately smoothed sand. Jaz and Jo ran down, threw off shoes and socks, and jumped waves, overcoming the sudden shyness of new friendship with a burst of silliness.

A watery sun was forcing its way through, low on the horizon, with a promise of being back tomorrow. Giant shadows stretched almost from one breakwater to the next. Jasmine thought of homework and the long walk home. 'I really ought to be going,' she said.

'Yeah, OK. Race ya.'

They ran, hobbling, slipping and sliding up mounds of pebbles, and sat on the kerb to put socks and shoes on damp and sandy feet.

'D'ya wanna ride my bike to the footbridge?'

Jaz leapt on and wobbled, unfamiliar with the bike, along the beach road and down across the green. Up on to the river path and she was gaining in confidence, streaking ahead towards the footbridge, while Jo puffed behind.

'Look out,' Jo yelled suddenly. Ahead, a bulky figure filled the narrow path. But it was too late. Jaz crashed cleanly and neatly into him. Bike and rider toppled, the man sprawled on the path, an armful of parcels and packets fell around him.

The man picked himself up stiffly and let forth a barrage of abuse.

Jo caught the tail end of it, as she rushed to the rescue. 'Flamin' blacks, can't get away from them. Even here. Always in the way.'

Jaz's mumbled apologies fell on deaf ears. She scrambled to pick up his scattered packets, but he snatched them away. He strode off, muttering, 'Stupid kid—not safe to be let out.'

'Did I hear him right?' Jo came puffing up.

Jaz's lip wobbled slightly.

'You OK?' asked Jo, still panting.

Jaz nodded and rubbed a grazed elbow. 'I haven't done anything to the bike, have I?'

Jo checked it over. 'No problem, it's tough, don't worry.'

But Jaz was staring thoughtfully at the receding figure of the man. 'I bet that's him. I bet that's the smuggler.'

'What?' Jo had not yet discovered that Jasmine's ambition, next to being a dancer, was to be a detective.

'Look, he had all those parcels, all carefully wrapped up. Did you see how he snatched them away? He didn't want me to touch them.'

Jo thought that had more to do with the colour of Jaz's skin, but she didn't like to say so.

'He came out of that house there. On the corner of the green—Number 23.'

They studied the house. It wasn't that far from *Trade Winds*, but Jo had never noticed it before. The curtains were firmly pulled. The paint on the windows was peeling and only a few windblown roses clung to life in the gravelled patch of garden. It didn't look sinister, merely dull and nondescript. The only sign of life was a handwritten note tacked to the gate:

FOR SALE
Mary Jane
Wayfarer Dinghy
Ideal for Trips on Sea or River
Enquire within

'Wow, I think you're right.' Now Jo was convinced. 'See that—*Mary Jane*.'

Jaz was uncomprehending. 'It's only a name.'

'It's slang for drugs—marijuana.'

'How d'you know?'

'I saw it on the telly, that New York programme—you know.'

Jaz didn't know, but it sounded convincing.

'And look at that. "Trips"—see, that's drugs.'

'But it says "Wayfarer Dinghy"—it's just a boat.'

'Nah, coded message, I bet. Wayfarer—that's like traveller. Lots of travellers take drugs.'

'Oh . . . I suppose it could be. Well, we'd better tell the police.' Jaz got on the bike as if about to pedal off to the copshop that moment.

'Hang on. You don't honestly think they'd believe us, do you? A couple of kids?'

'No . . . I s'pose not . . .' Jaz dismounted. 'Well, we'll just have to find some proof, then.' A determined look came over her face. 'Tell you what, why don't we keep watch, shadow his movements, stake him out—that's what all the best detectives do.'

'Yeah, I've seen that on telly too,' said Jo, less than enthusiastic. 'You don't mean now, do you?'

'No, silly, I've got to get home—and anyway, he's gone. How about Saturday? I bet that's his busy day. I'll come over in the morning and we can hide somewhere and keep watch.'

Jo sighed, it sounded a daft idea to her. But Jaz's enthusiasm was hard to resist, and Saturdays were pretty boring. 'OK, but not if it's raining.'

Saturday dawned fresh and golden, so there was no excuse.

'Grief, Jo, you're up early. Can you go down the town for me?' asked Mum, hunched in her dressing-gown over a coffee mug.

'Sorry, I've gotta meet someone.' And Jo skipped out before Mum could enquire too closely.

She met Jaz by the swings as arranged. They had decided to watch from the grassy bank sloping up from the green to the raised river path. From there they could get a good view of the smuggler's house, without being too obvious.

Jaz had come prepared, with a box of homemade flapjacks, a Walkman, some of her favourite tapes and a pair of binoculars. It was warm in the sun and they settled down to watch.

The house was as bleak as ever. Nothing moved. They stared at it, and at the river beyond with its bobbing yachts. In the distance they could see the power station chimney, a landmark for miles around. Clouds travelled the sky, their shadows racing with them over the ground.

It was easy to talk as they lay in the grass. They discussed the relative merits of their favourite groups, and Jaz confided her great ambition—or one of them, anyway——to be a dancer. Her shyness gradually fell away and she began to tell Jo about life in Birmingham. Tuesday afternoon tap and modern at Dorothy Thompson's Stage School, Yo-Yo's on Friday evening . . .

'Yo-Yo's?' queried Jo.

'Youth Group,' explained Jaz. 'It was part of the church.'

'Oh, church,' said Jo, dismissively.

'No, it was good.' Jaz tried to explain: Sunday mornings with hundreds of people crammed into a school hall, the worship band that was more like a rock group, with all ages, all nationalities, clapping and dancing together.

'That's some wacky church,' said Jo.

'It's a bit different here, though,' sighed Jaz. 'Harbour Street Chapel must've been exactly the same for about a hundred years. I think some of the people have been there that long.'

Then Jo described her life in London. The tall, thin terraced house, visits to the dingy club where Dad rehearsed his jazz band, the music and laughter when Mum and Dad had their friends round for drinks—— back when . . . Suddenly she found herself explaining all about Dad, about the day when the rows finally stopped and there was a gap on the shelves where his books ought to be. Jo had never told anyone before, but there was something about this Jaz. She didn't say a lot, but you could tell she was . . . sort of 'real', clear straight through. You didn't have to make yourself look good.

By eleven o'clock there had been no movement and Jo was beginning to get restless. 'We've been here hours,' she said.

'One hour, 58 minutes,' corrected Jaz.

'Nothing's gonna happen. Let's go round the shops.'

'Ssh, look!' Jaz grabbed the binoculars.

The door was opening and the smuggler coming out. Jo could swear he looked shiftily round to see if anyone was about.

'He's got something,' she whispered.

The man carried a black plastic sack. He took it to a bent and rusty bin and threw it in. Then he went back into the house and firmly shut the door behind him.

'Great, he emptied the rubbish. High spot of our day.'

'No, that's very important. Why didn't I think of that? You could get a lot of clues from rubbish.'

'Yeah, about yesterday's dinner. That's all. Drugs don't come in printed packets, y'know. "New Improved Crack—special offer, 4p off".'

'Under cover of darkness would be best. You could come back and do it this evening.'

'Oh yeah. You must be joking.'

A few kids played football on the green, a motor boat hummed up the narrow river channel. The clock struck half past eleven, seagulls wheeled lazily, and only a few crumbs remained of the flapjacks.

The thud of running feet made Jo and Jaz turn. They got a good view of some tanned muscled legs, and then eyes, blue as the sky, looking down at them. The eyes were startled by their heads popping up in the grass, but the startled look quickly gave way to a smile that would melt butter. 'Hi, girls.' Then he was gone. They stared as the young jogger went on his way, blond hair flipping from side to side.

'He's a bit nice.'

'I like the legs.'

'Y'know, I do prefer older men,' said Jaz, thinking of a certain seventeen-year-old she had worshipped from afar and left behind in Birmingham.

'Yeah, all the boys our age are brain-dead and covered in zits.' They agreed this as an accurate assessment of all second- and third-year males at Downview Comprehensive, and settled down again to watch. Nothing happened. A light aircraft buzzed overhead. A dog barked. Jo's stomach rumbled. The sun was lulling them into a gentle doze, when: 'Hang about, here we go.'

The man was coming out again. This time he was going somewhere—and he had a parcel under his arm.

'There you are. Did you see how shiftily he looked round? Come on, let's follow him.'

But Jo had kicked her trainers off and was scrabbling to find them in the long grass.

'Oh—come on,' wailed Jaz. 'Well, I'm going anyway, you stay and keep watch.'

Jaz set off looking very much like someone trying to look casual.

Jo tied her laces and wondered whether to run after her. 'S'pose I'd better.' She glanced at the house as she passed. Funny, it looked as if the door was still ajar. She stopped. Here was her chance to do some real detective work.

Jo went up to the door—working out a line about looking for sponsors for a charity swim, just in case there was someone there. She hesitated, rehearsing her sponsor speech, then knocked.

No answer—or was there a faint muffled sound somewhere? She tried again. Silence. She pushed the door and tried to accustom her eyes to the gloom. She was in a living-room: a flickering TV in the corner, a table covered with boxes and packing, and a pile of cash. There was definitely something going on here. She was advancing to the table when an angry howl from the room beyond raised the hairs on her arms and pinned her feet to the floor.

A figure rushed in, arms flailing. It was a boy, about her age, holding something in one hand. The next moment the something was flying through the air towards her. She ducked and it hit the wall with a metallic crash, releasing a shower of small objects. The boy gave a cry and flung himself on the floor, scrabbling to gather them and stuff them in his mouth.

Jo edged forwards nervously, for he was crouched between her and the door. Her movement made the boy start and he looked up, staring with wild eyes. Jo stared back. Then she smiled. The missile was a tin and the hail of shrapnel was toffees, which had burst out as the lid flew off.

The boy smiled back.

He advanced toward her, dribbling, and grabbed her arm. He led her towards the packages on the table. He seemed to want to show her them and was evidently pleased when she reached out and took one. Jo was pleased when he released his tight grip. He offered her a toffee.

'Er, yeah, well, nice to meet ya . . . Thanks a lot, that's great . . .'

She backed towards the door. The boy advanced towards her, arms waving clumsily and holding out another toffee. She turned, ready to run, and glanced through the open door—and there was the smuggler coming along the river path towards her.

She turned again, ready to try a back door, but the boy barred her way.

Any minute the smuggler would see her. She was trapped!

3

Artists in Residence

The smuggler had something under his arm. 'A gun!'
thought Jo in panic. As he strolled along he began to
draw it out ... It was nothing more sinister than a
rolled-up newspaper. Jo saw him glance down at the
headlines—and took her chance.

'Bye, mate,' she said to the strange boy, as she
prepared to dash across the front yard to the safety of
the path.

The man hadn't seen her yet—but Jaz, still following behind, had. She acted quickly—a routine worthy
of Dorothy Thompson's stage school. 'Oooh, ouch,
owww.' Jaz writhed in agony on the path. The man
turned to see the disturbance, and Jo dashed out of the
house and on to the path.

'What's up?' asked the man, looming over Jaz as she
lay on the path.

'Ow, oo, er ... my leg hurts.'

'Oh, it's you,' he scowled. 'Let's have a look, then.'
He reluctantly bent to help.

She looked round. Jo had disappeared. 'Er, it's
feeling better now. I'll just try standing on it,' said
Jaz hastily, scrambling to her feet.

'Is that your idea of a joke? Flamin' blacks! What is it with you people?' And with a stream of abuse, he turned and strode off towards his house.

Jaz heaved a sigh, too relieved to worry about the insults, and noticed how much her heart was pounding.

She made her way past the smuggler's house, remembering to limp. The curtains stayed shut. Twenty metres further up the path, she scuttled down the slope to the green. Under cover of the bank she doubled back, expecting to find Jo at their look-out post.

There was no sign of her. Jaz sank down on the grass, wondering what to do next. She stayed there until her heart stopped thumping and then, puzzled, retraced her steps.

'Pssst.' Jo's voice came from nowhere. 'I'm over here.'

Jo had decided in her dash to make for the nearest hiding-place—straight across the path into a ram-shackle shed that belonged to the houseboat opposite. She crouched there now on a pile of driftwood. Jaz slipped in to join her.

'Is it . . . ?'

'It's all right, this boat's been empty for ages.'

Jaz glanced nervously out at the boat. True, there were no signs of life: no geraniums in pots, no bikes, no lines of washing—nothing to mark it out as inhabited at all. Its name sign, *Shangri-La*, hung tipsily from one nail.

'Well?' asked Jo.

'He went to the Post Office,' reported Jaz, 'and bought a paper and a quarter of Pontefract-cakes. He

31

posted the parcel . . . And now he recognizes me. He called me . . . names. Didn't get us very far, did it?'

'Bloomin' cheek.'

'Never mind that. What on earth were you doing?'

'Well, the door was open so I thought I'd go and see, and there's this really weird boy in there . . . But look, I got this.' And Jo held aloft a brown paper packet in triumph.

'But that's stealing.' Jaz looked indignant.

'Oh good grief, how else could we find out? I risk life and limb . . .'

'*You* risk life and limb?'

'Yeah, well, thanks for rescuing me. That was a good bit of acting.'

'I don't think it fooled him . . . Oh, come on. Now you've got it, you'd better open it.'

They were too busy fumbling with sellotape and brown paper to notice the soft padding footsteps, until a shadow fell across the open doorway of the shed. They found themselves facing a bronzed pair of legs. The blond jogger stood over them—angry, Jaz thought—but when he spoke his voice was controlled and friendly. 'Now what exactly are you doing?'

'Er, we're hiding.'

'From our friends,' added Jo.

'So where are they, then?' asked the jogger with a smile, surveying the empty path and the distant green.

'I expect they're hiding too. It's a spying game,' Jo improvised.

'Well, girls, you can spy on me any time . . . But not on my property.'

'Sorry. We thought this one was empty. D'ya live here then?' asked Jo, suddenly curious.

32

'Yes, I've owned it for a while, but I'm not often here. Too much travelling. I've been in the States a lot of the time, or I've had business that's kept me in London. But I'll be here a little more now—and I don't want trespassers!' The smile remained fixed, but the message was clear.

'No, right, sorry.' The girls backed off. Still glancing nervously over their shoulders they made their way to the safety of *Trade Winds*.

'I bet he's a pop star,' said Jo.

'Or an actor.'

'He's real good-looking.'

'He was nice, wasn't he, considering we were trespassing?'

Two lots of trespassing in one day, thought Jaz. Perhaps this wasn't such a good idea.

'So what about this packet then?' It had been forgotten, but Jo still clutched it in a sweaty hand. One tug released the sellotape. They both held their breath. Was this the vital evidence they needed?

'Christmas cards!'

'Bit out of season,' commented Mum vaguely, passing through the cabin with a basketful of washing.

'Drugs smuggler—my elbow,' said Jo, when Mum was out of earshot.

Jaz shook them, looked in the envelopes hopefully, but Christmas cards they were. Bright ones, pretty ones, simple designs made from children's drawings—but no drugs.

'Suspicious character, huh?'

'However can we explain?' asked Jaz.

'Explain?' queried Jo.

'When we take them back.'

33

'Take them back! You must be kidding.' But Jo had a horrible feeling that Jaz wasn't kidding at all. 'Look, I told you, there's that weird boy in there.'

'What sort of weird?'

'Well, peculiar, a bit simple.'

'Was he dangerous, shackled to the floor or something?'

'No—not exactly. He threw a tin of toffees at me, but it missed.'

'So what's the problem? Come on.'

Jo tried another tack. 'Look, they had stacks of these packets. They'll never miss one.'

'It's stealing.'

'Well ... we had our reasons. Anyway, they're no use to us ...'

'It's still stealing.' There was a heavy pause. 'What if we say that we ...'

'*We* say?' Jo was having no part in this.

'Well, you took them.'

'Look, Father Christmas 'imself wouldn't drag me in there.'

There was a long silence while Jaz debated with herself. Jo kept quiet and hoped she'd given up the idea.

Finally Jaz picked up the cards. 'OK, I'll go,' she said, and marched resolutely out.

That's all I need—a detective with a conscience, thought Jo. Unwillingly she got up. 'Hang on, I'm comin',' she called.

The smuggler's house was still curtained and shut up. Their timid knock seemed to echo around the estuary and right over to the Downs. Jo hoped against hope that no one was in.

But of course someone was. The smuggler himself

came to the door, with the weird boy hovering in the background.

'Yes?' said the man with a look which said, 'You again'.

Jaz forced the words out. 'It's about the cards.'

'What? Oh, you mean the advert in the paper.'

The words 'What advert?' were forming on Jaz's lips, but Jo was too quick for her. 'Yes, that's right, the advert.'

'Well, you look a bit young, but I suppose we can't be choosy,' said the man reluctantly. 'We need all the help we can get. You'd better come in.' In the background the boy shuffled from foot to foot, hiding his eyes and moaning slightly. It wasn't exactly a warm welcome, but Jaz thought she'd better accept.

'So, have you sold charity cards before?'

Jaz's mouth dropped but Jo filled the silence. 'No, but we'd love to 'ave a go. I'm sure we'd be good at it.'

'Hmm, well, I'll get you a form to fill in.' The man turned away and Jo saw her chance. She grabbed the package that Jaz was still holding behind her back and returned it to the table it had come from half an hour earlier.

'No confessions,' she hissed in Jaz's ear.

'No, we don't do collections,' said the man turning back. 'The association prefers to sell its own work. Have you seen the cards?'

And again the cards were picked up from the table.

'Yes, we have actually,' said Jaz to Jo's horror. 'They're very nice.'

'All done by children from Headstart.' The man spread them out. Some of the pictures showed a degree of skill, but most were the kind of simple stick men

35

pictures that primary children turn out. The man picked up the simplest of them all, just a few splodges of colour of the sort that are pinned up in nurseries or framed in galleries of modern art.

'Gary did that.' The man turned to the drooling boy, and for a moment his cold face lit up. 'My son.'

'It's good,' said Jaz politely.

The boy moved closer to Jaz and stared blankly at her. 'It's very good,' she repeated to him, but he seemed not to have heard. Suddenly his hand darted up to her face. She flinched, thinking he might hit her, but in the gentlest manner possible he fingered her plaited hair.

'Gary, leave her alone,' said the man sharply.

'It's all right.' Jaz smiled at the boy and there was the faintest flicker of a response.

'No, no.' The man grabbed Gary's hand. He seemed angry. The boy whimpered and retreated, confused. His father clumsily tried to comfort him.

He mumbled an apology, avoiding Jaz's eyes. He handed the form past her to Jo. 'I don't think you're quite what we're looking for, but fill it in and we'll see.'

He opened the door, to show that the visit was over. Jaz and Jo had no wish to prolong it either.

'Right, thanks. Bye,' and they were dashing along the path to *Trade Winds*.

Mum wasn't there. 'Gone for a half at the Ship,' said the note on the kitchen table.

But Abby was, hunched up on the bench seat, clutching a mug of tea. 'This is my sister,' said Jo with the same note of family pride that the smuggler had used of his dribbling son.

To Jaz's eyes it was just as misplaced. The girl in the

window-seat looked listless and vacant. Jo, too familiar with her to notice, saw only the brilliant art student. But Abby, aroused, changed instantly from a tired caterpillar to a brilliant butterfly.

'Jo, sis!... What's doin'?... Who's your friend?... Hi, great name... I'm Abigail, awful name, call me Abby... So what've you been up to then?'

'Don't ask,' said Jo, rummaging through a cupboard. 'Want some cornflakes?'

Cornflakes seemed an odd lunch to Jaz, but she was hungry enough for anything.

'Nah, no milk. Never any milk. What about toast?'

In the end they managed baked beans and fried eggs—the odd bits of shell didn't matter that much.

Abby was hungry too. But even as she wolfed down the food, her movements were graceful. Abby was the sort of person people stared at in bus queues, and Jaz found herself staring too. Her hair was black and spiky and her ears jangled with a whole row of silver earrings. She wore black velvet, with a vivid yellow scarf. She sat upright now, cross-legged and straight-backed. When she had cleared her plate, she launched into a description of her latest project—a set of stage designs for *Coriolanus*. Jaz had no idea what Corio-whatsit was, but she listened, fascinated. Abby had the knack of drawing you in, making you feel she valued your opinion.

'So what about my party then?' She switched subjects abruptly. 'You gotta come, sis. You can both come. You'll come, won't you, Jaz? There's a few decent guys you might like. And we've got this crazy DJ.'

Jaz was flattered. She felt that there was no one in the world Abby wanted to her party more than her.

Abby tried Jo again. 'Look, Mum'll let you. You're not a kid any more. You could stay over. It won't finish till morning anyway, but don't tell Mum that.'

'I didn't understand all that about the cards, did you?' asked Jaz later as she and Jo wandered back towards the town.

They had given Abby their promise to come next Saturday, and Jo had also given her £8.20, all her worldly wealth, with the promise of its return next Saturday and a flashing smile. Abby had left in a rush.

'Nah, not really,' Jo pondered the card saga again. 'What was that application form anyway?' She fished the folded paper from her pocket. 'Headstart,' she read. 'An association for the families of brain-damage victims. Help fund research and provide support by promoting our wide range of Christmas and birthday cards. Sell to your friends and neighbours, and work colleagues. Why not organize a party-plan sale? NB: All volunteer sales staff must be over sixteen.'

'Oh dear, we won't be able to do it, then. What a shame.' Jo's heavy wit bounced off Jaz without a trace.

'Yes, it is a shame. That poor boy.'

Jaz and Jo wandered round the shops in uneasy silence. Both were feeling a little foolish about their morning's activity.

'Dunno how you can believe in God,' said Jo abruptly as they were trying lipsticks in the chemist's.

Jaz flushed with embarrassment. 'Why not?'

'Well, it's not fair, is it? There's people like my sister and that jogger. They look good and they're successful and all. And then there's people like that boy Gary and 'is grouchy Dad.' Jo didn't add, 'Not to mention me,' but she thought it. She sighed as she considered the pink lipstick, and the face surrounding it. It wasn't a bad face, a bit on the round side, eyes of no special colour and unruly ginger hair. But Jo, facing herself in the mirror, had no doubt which category she was in. 'It's not fair.'

Jaz looked troubled. She had to agree. It wasn't fair. She wanted to defend God. She believed in him. She'd grown up believing. But somehow she couldn't find the right words. Her stammered attempt: 'Well, God loves everyone,' came out as a goody-goody stupid thing to say and met only with a 'Big deal' from Jo.

'Aw, come on,' said Jo after a minute. 'Let's try that new discount store. Nothin' like a good bargain to cheer yerself up.'

4

Party Animals

'Oh no, it looks really awful.'

Jaz stripped off the skimpy sweater and flung it on to an ever-growing pile of clothes on the bed.

Jo looked on in amazement. How could Jaz be so incredibly fussy? She looked good in almost anything.

But Jo had to admit that Jaz had good reason—tonight was the night of the party. Amazingly, everyone had agreed. With a little help from the time-honoured tactic of 'Everyone else is allowed...', both Pastor and Mrs Walcott and Maggie Thomas had given in.

The Walcotts had surprised Jaz with their willingness. Yes, they were anxious, and if they had known more about student parties they might have been more so, but that was balanced by an even greater anxiety that their daughter should not be lonely.

'It's one thing for us to uproot and follow the Lord's will,' Mrs Walcott had remarked to her husband, 'but it's not so easy on the kids.'

Jasmine hadn't said much about her first days at school, and Mrs Walcott suspected the going was tough. But this Jodi girl had taken her under her wing, and that had made all the difference. The family seemed a bit odd, living on a houseboat, but the Walcotts would have lived in a tent if the Lord had told them to, and being conventional wasn't high on their list of essentials.

So going to this girl's sister's party seemed like quite a good idea. ('Everyone my age goes to parties,' said Jaz, not mentioning that no one else her age except Jo was going to this one.) But there was one condition.

'I'll pick you up at eleven o'clock,' said Dad.

'Midnight,' said Jaz, and a heated bargaining session brought it to eleven-thirty as everyone knew it would. Jaz admitted to herself that Dad, with his mind on tomorrow morning's sermon, was being very generous.

If a Reverend would let his thirteen-year-old go to a student party, then Maggie Thomas could hardly refuse. Besides, as it happened, that Saturday was the opening of the East Sussex Artists' Guild annual exhibition, and social events for Maggie were few and far between.

'Abby says I can stay the night,' said Jo, expecting a 'No chance' reply. What she didn't know about was a certain Martin Tewson-Smith, widower and painter of insipid water colours. Had she known, she would have said, 'Mum, what a drip.' Martin Tewson-Smith had one of those awful little moustaches that look like a toothbrush. Maggie didn't like the moustache much either, but its owner had been friendly and Maggie was lonely. So when Jo suggested staying in Brighton, Maggie thought of a intimate late-night supper for two at *Trade Winds* and . . . 'Mmm, all right. Get back for lunch on Sunday. Your Dad's coming to take you out.'

'Oh, great,' said Jo flatly. She loved Dad, course she did. He was fun, a good laugh. Why did she always feel bad when he came? Still, at least he wasn't around to get all heavy-handed about her going out. Sometimes he still treated her like a little kid.

And so, one way and another, the parent hurdle had been overcome. Here was the next—what to wear. Jo had decided T-shirt and jeans. That wasn't difficult, it was what she always wore. Which T-shirt had been a matter of some discussion, and there had been several hours of experimenting with hair gel and drier, and putting on and rubbing off eye pencil. But now Jo was ready and it was only Jaz who was being difficult.

It wasn't as if she hadn't had a choice. Jo had offered her a shirt of hers, a few of Abby's cast-offs and even some jewellery of her Mum's. Jaz had been to Oxfam, the Legion Jumble and Brighton market, and she still wasn't sure. In fact with her deep coffee colouring and slender figure she looked good in all of them, but 'Too childish', 'Too old-fashioned', 'Too big', 'Too small' had been her verdict on one outfit after the other.

At last she had decided. A skimpy skirt from the market, one of Abby's old tops and a leather jacket from Oxfam, her own boots and Maggie Thomas's huge hoop earrings.

'You look seriously stylish,' said Jo, and she seriously meant it.

It was perhaps a good thing that the Walcotts had gone to a Gospel Rally in Horsham and were not there to see their sweet little Jasmine transformed into the streetwise thirteen-going-on-seventeen Jaz and boarding the 8.30 Brighton bus for a night on the town.

You could hear the music from the end of the street.

'Hey, kid! Mum let you come then. You look great.' This last remark addressed to Jaz, Abby drew them in with one of her ice-melting smiles. 'Come and get a drink. And something to eat while you can. There's not much of that.'

She drew them past the living-room, gloomy with a single red lightbulb. Despite the pounding beat, only a few figures stood motionless around the walls. 'It's really early yet,' bellowed Abby above the noise. 'Most people come after the pubs close.'

They followed her into a minute kitchen where a keg of beer, some cartons of wine, stacks of six-packs and a long tube of paper cups stood in readiness.

Food was Tandoori chicken chunks, pitta bread, some unidentifiable dips and a huge bowl of peanuts. Jo, who hadn't had anything since a bowl of Weetabix at 12.30, grabbed a handful of peanuts and a chicken wing. Jaz dipped the pitta into some pink stuff and hoped it was all right. 'Taramasalata,' said Abby. It could have been the name of a rock group, an introduction to the Indian guy in the corner, or a student greeting. Jaz didn't know so she just said, 'Yeah, great,' and 'Hi' towards the corner, and hoped that covered it. But Abby was already rushing to answer the ringing doorbell. Last night's washing-up was still in the sink, noticed Jaz, the rubbish bin was overflowing and the clock stood at 9.03.

The clock crept round to 10.03, but the party stood still. A few people trickled in. They gathered around the drinks and totally ignored Jaz and Jo. Jaz was wishing she hadn't pushed Dad for the unheard-of lateness of 11.30, and Jo was struggling with embarrassment that her sister had so few friends.

Not that Abby was bothered. 'They'll turn up soon,' she said, and, sure enough, by 10.30 a steady stream of Brighton's young began to pour through the door. Some were scruffy, some glittering, some drab, some outrageous—to Jo they all seemed full of that magic quality, 'Life'. There wasn't any of the capital 'L' stuff in Shoreham, of course, but here, as the laughter got louder along with the music, was a glimpse of it.

In the living-room, bodies started moving. A tall blond guy, the scruffy sort, grabbed Jaz and took her to dance. Jo watched, half-disgruntled, half-proud that her friend was such a good dancer that others turned to look.

Jo watched from the doorway and waited for some-one to ask her to show her dancing skills. But no one did and the longer she stood there, the more awkward she felt. People began to push past her, they stood in front of her, talked over her—and at last she fled to the kitchen. So she didn't see when another guy, the drab sort, pulled Jaz close to him.

Jaz only had time to see that he was dark-eyed, pale-skinned and mysterious, before someone dimmed the lights to nothing. She noticed he wore a strange cross earring. Perhaps he was religious. They swayed rhythmically in the dark. Was this her big chance, wondered Jaz, and snuggled closer. She couldn't lean her head on his shoulder (he was a little bit short, she admitted) but he leaned his on hers—well, her front really, and his chin was rough and stubbly.

Only a red glow from the disco unit lit the room. It was crowded, loud and hot. Jaz fought back a faint and really stupid panic. People kept bumping into her, touching her. No, it was his hands—moving to places she wasn't sure she wanted them to go.

Was he carried away with uncontrollable passion? She looked at him, expecting a romantic look, a whispered word or two, but he looked absent-minded, bored even, and smiled sheepishly.

He held her tighter, staring into space, and together they swayed to the beat, hemmed in by other swaying couples.

Jaz looked around helplessly for Jo. Her place in the doorway was empty. Jaz felt a hot flush of panic. With her arm round pale-and-mysterious' neck she looked at her watch—11.15.

'Hallelujah,' she thought, and almost laughed out loud.

Pale-and-mysterious looked at her intensely. 'D'you know you've got beautiful vibrations?' he murmured. 'A wonderful aura. What sign are you?'

'Sign?'

'I'm Taurus. How about you?'

'Um, I'm not sure, I don't know ... I've got to find my friend, go to the loo ...'

She pulled herself away from him and pushed through the crush, stepping over couples lining the corridor and stairs. She kicked over a glass half-full of beer. It trickled step by step down the stairs. Someone swore but no one bothered to stop it. She found a tissue and tried to mop it up, but they told her to stop fussing.

She searched everywhere for Jo. Where was she? Then she found the loo. A girl was standing in front smoking. Jaz waited her turn politely, but whoever was inside was taking an awful long time. She noticed that the door wasn't locked.

'Excuse me, are you in a queue?'

The girl looked at her blankly, laughed wildly and blew strange sweet smoke in her face. She continued to lean on the door. Jaz pushed round her and opened the door. The girl flopped aside like a rag doll.

The loo was a safe haven. Jaz locked the door and sat down—relieved in more ways than one. 11.23. Could she stay there for seven minutes without anyone noticing? The walls were painted dark blue and pasted with magazine cuttings, postcards and drawings. Peacocks on a lawn, the intricate inside of a mosque, theatre sketches, starving African babies, one of those drawings with stairs that when you followed them round and round went nowhere.

For six minutes Jaz stared at the images that inspired Abby's art. They were beautiful but to Jaz they all seemed unreal. But perhaps it was only the thump of music and the blue-shaded light that made her feel that way.

It was 11.28. She decided to bolt for it. Jo was still nowhere to be seen. Abby passed by.

'Tell Jo I've gone,' shouted Jaz but she didn't hear.

Outside the rainy street seemed almost peaceful. She tugged down her skirt and buttoned her jacket to the neck. The noise was distant now. It sounded like the sort of party you wished you were at. A tatty old Vauxhall came up the street, and Jaz thought it was the most comforting car in the whole world.

If Dad noticed the skirt and the make-up he made no comment. 'Had a good time, angel?' he asked.

'Yeah, Dad, it was brilliant,' answered Jaz.

Jo, after her flight from the sitting-room, had first made for Abby's bedroom. She thought she would just put on a bit more make-up and do her hair. But a crowd was lounging over Abby's duvet, listening to a girl holding forth about rainforests, Indians and respect for the wilderness. They were passing round some white powder and sniffing it.

She backed out. In the kitchen, they were discussing travel. Names like Budapest, Los Angeles, and Samarkand were tossed about. Jo wondered whether her school trip to Paris would fit the conversation, but decided against it.

Abby passed by her, arm round a Chinese boy. 'Jo, babe. Having a good time?' Abby seemed faintly surprised to see her.

Jo found herself alone in a flat full of people, none of whom was the least bit interested in her.

She ducked drinks, stepped over legs and squirmed between bodies to the door at the end of the corridor. Thankfully she pulled back the bolt and slipped outside to the iron fire-escape.

Beyond the dark rooftops the lights of Brighton glittered. A cool breeze soothed Jo's burning face. Somewhere a blackbird sang, out of time with the pounding beat inside. A cat slunk across the lawn below. The garden smelt of fresh-cut grass and recent showers. Jo sat on the steps and a new awareness crept over her——the steps were wet.

She also became aware of movement behind her. Someone else was sharing her secret place. She glimpsed skinny knees in torn jeans, but the voice

47

still made her jump.

> *The long day wanes: the slow moon climbs:*
> *The deep moans round with many voices.*
> *Come, my friends—'tis not too late to seek a newer*
> *   world . . .*

'Alfred Lord Tennyson. D'you like poetry?'

'Er, sort of, I dunno much.'

There was a scrabbling in the corner. She made out a scraggy face, framed by dark curls. The light caught something in the boy's hand. It was a syringe. Horrified, Jo watched him put it down, rub his arm and roll down his sleeve. 'Terrible—don't ever do it. Hi, I'm Dimitri—Dim for short.'

He held out the hand at the end of the arm, Jo took it, automatically polite.

'Hey, the moon—it's almost full.'

Jo looked up to see the moon burst from the scattering cloud. Way out over the sea's hidden presence, one bright star blinked. She turned back, 'D'you take drugs?'

'Very observant.' He was still grasping her hand.

'Why?'

'Seeking a newer world . . . I dunno. Looking for something, I suppose. I'm not addicted. It's just a good feeling . . . But don't start, kid.' He peered at her. 'You are a kid, aren't you?'

'I'm fourteen.'

'Bit young for this kind of party.'

'I'm Abby's sister. Are you an art student too?'

'Me? No, couldn't draw a pint of beer. I'm at the University, doing English. Don't ask me why.'

'Why not?'

'Why not! D'you know what they suggest I do after this? Be a civil servant. Or teach. God help us. Meanwhile I'm drowning in a sea of words—dissertations, recitations, phonetics, polemics, Renaissance, Romantics...'

'I don't like school, either.'

'So what you going to do with your life, kid—whatever-your-name-is?'

'Jo. I dunno... Help people, have fun.'

'Hope you do, kid. Find a newer world. Perhaps you can.'

He loosened his grip on her hand and stared at the moon. His fingers tapped out the distant rhythm.

'D'you know lots of poetry?' queried Jo.

'Yeah, tons and tons.'

'D'you write any?'

'There was a young lady from Brighton, Who jumped into bed with the light on... Only that sort of thing.'

'That's the sort I understand. What's the end?'

He was silent for a while.

'She said, "In the dark It's much more of a lark... but I'm much too easily frightened".'

'That's good.'

'Not quite Tennyson.' Dimitri's eyelids were falling. His voice seemed to come from a long way off.

> *My life has crept so long on a broken wing*
> *Through cells of madness, haunts of horror*
> *   and fear*
> *That I come to be grateful at last for a little thing...*

He picked up the spent syringe and broke the needle. 'Like this,' he said.

They sat in silence for a long, long while. Down in the town a police siren wailed. Shrieks of laughter came from the kitchen. The blackbird sang again. Dimitri slumped against the railings.

Jo shivered. She had a sudden fear he might die while she sat there. She leaned closer. He was still breathing. She tried to pull him inside. He muttered something and pushed her away. Still she pulled, she must get him away from the railings. He opened his eyes and smiled.

'What's the problem, kid?'

'You might fall.'

'No problem. Nice to know you care.'

He shuffled nearer to the wall and with a desperate shove Jo wedged him into a corner.

'OK, OK, now gimme some peace.'

He closed his eyes. The moon went in, and a breeze rustled the elm trees. Jo shivered. Dimitri seemed to be sleeping peacefully.

Eventually and reluctantly she went inside. The party was dying down. A few couples lined the stairs. Half a dozen diehards were still dancing in the living-room. From the loo came the unmistakable sound of someone throwing up. There were two people on Abby's bed. She didn't stop to see what they were doing. There was no sign of Abby.

The kitchen was deserted, a whirlpool of paper cups, empty bottles and cans. Absently Jo scooped some of the dip with her fingers. Suddenly she felt very hungry and picked the bowls clean of their few remaining crisps, bread and chicken wings.

The laughter was coming from Abby's flatmate's room. She pushed open the door. A crowd of people sat around a single candle. One girl, a scarf tied round her head gypsy-fashion, was reading a palm. 'I see a beautiful life...' Cheers. 'And lots of children...' Groans. 'But the line breaks suddenly. I see life cut short.' 'Rubbish,' said the owner of the palm, and withdrew it.

In the corner a thin boy with long straggly hair started to pass something round the room. Each person sniffed at the powder through a straw, snorting some up in one swooping movement. Jo's eyes followed its progress until she realized Abby was right near her, sitting behind the door. She watched her take the powder and follow the same ritual. Jo waited to see if it made her spaced-out like Dimitri, but she just seemed brighter and bouncier than normal. Someone cracked a corny joke and they all laughed as if it were the funniest thing in the world.

The clock said 01.43. Someone turned up the music. Jo slipped out and closed the door. Jaz must have gone long since. She wished she hadn't said she'd stay the night. She was tired and there was nowhere to sleep.

'Blow that. I'm not stayin' up all night.'

In the living-room the chairs were piled in a corner. She pulled the cushions off and took them into the hall. She opened the hall cupboard and looked inside. Great—she was right—a sleeping bag. And Abby's old fur coat. She dragged them all down the landing and into the bathroom, locked the door and settled down for a night in the bath.

5

Saturday Night
and Sunday Morning

Jo awoke, aching, in the grey dawn. Her watch said 5.30. All was silent. She levered herself stiffly out of the bath and tiptoed through the flat. A couple were sleeping entwined on the landing. She stepped over them. In the living-room the red-shaded light still glowed. Three girls were sleeping on the floor, a guy on the sofa.

With a pang of worry Jo remembered Dimitri. A girl was propped in front of the fire escape door, eyes half-open. Jo pushed her gently. With a moan she toppled to one side. Jo prised open the door and slipped outside. There was no one there. She looked down, half expecting to see a body spread-eagled below. There was nothing.

Course not, stupid, she told herself. Dimitri was probably home in bed right now, sleeping off one night's silly experiment.

The garden was grey, drained of colour, but alive with sound. The unseen birds were going crazy, joyously celebrating a new day. Over the rooftops, the sky was golden. Somewhere, out beyond the hotels and chalk cliffs, the sun was already shining on the sea. Jo shivered and went back indoors.

Back in her bathroom sanctuary, she thought of going back to sleep, but knew she couldn't. Her face peered at her from the mirror. Experimental make-up sat in big smudges beneath her eyes. She ran the tap and splashed her face. The water was cold, there was no flannel and the smudges wouldn't go.

She opened Abby's bathroom cabinet—maybe there would be eye make-up remover. Aspirins, deodorant, shower gel. She moved a ball of tissue in her search. Something heavy fell from it and she was vaguely surprised to recognize the gold and ruby antique ring that Mum had inherited from Aunt Ethel. Mum always said it was the only valuable thing she possessed. She'd never said she'd given it to Abby. But Jo's musings were cut short when she pushed aside a shampoo bottle. Behind it was a syringe.

She stared at it blankly for a moment, until realization dawned and a tremor of shock ran through her. This couldn't be Abby's cabinet. It must belong to her flatmate. She opened the other cabinet, searched for proof—she found only the red hair dye that was Mel's trademark.

Jo looked back at the syringe. Some small wrapped packets lay beside it. She picked one up—a needle. Next to them she recognized the peppermint foot lotion and strawberry bath oil she had given Abby for Christmas.

Jo shut the cabinet and her smudged face came into view again. She soaped the corner of a towel and scrubbed her eyes furiously. There was a perfectly

53

logical explanation, she was sure. There must be all sorts of things people use syringes for. She couldn't think of any.

Jo rushed out of the bathroom. She wanted to talk to Abby, to reassure herself. But Abby lay sleeping, fully clothed, on her bed. A guy Jo had never met before lay nuzzled up to her.

'Abby.' Jo tried to wake her.

Abby turned over, groaning slightly. The guy turned too and threw his arm around her. His eyes opened slightly. 'Whaddaya want?' he muttered.

'Er, nothing. Tell Abby I've gone home.'

Jo ran down the stairs and out of Flat C. She pushed past the bikes in the communal corridor and stepped over the junk mail that no one ever opened. The main front door creaked shut behind her and she was out in the sunlit street.

There weren't many buses, she discovered, at six o'clock on a Sunday morning. But she wasn't going back and she wasn't going to sit in the bus shelter for two hours. There was nothing for it but to walk the six miles back to Shoreham.

Her brain pounded an insistent rhythm as she walked. What about Abby? What about Abby? Tiredness came over her in waves. She had seen a side of her sister she didn't know, and it frightened her.

But gradually the morning worked its magic. The sea broke in bursts of white foam and drew back with a clatter over the freshly-scoured shingle. A raindrop glistened at the heart of each marigold in the municipal flower-beds, and Brighton seemed like a world newly-created. True, there was still litter on the promenade, rust on the railings, graffiti in the shelters, but mornings like this made you believe in new starts.

It was just a phase. Abby would get over it. Dad was coming down today. It was ages since they'd seen him. Perhaps one day they'd be a family again. As she put one weary foot in front of the other, she began to feel better.

By 7.45 she was on the outskirts of Shoreham. People were beginning to stir, walking their dogs and collecting newspapers. She noticed someone she recognized striding along. It was Jaz's dad.

Had anything happened to Jaz? Where had she got to last night? He crossed the road and strode towards Jo. Was he out looking for her, to tell her off for leading his daughter astray?

For a moment her heart lurched, but suddenly he turned aside. She realized he hadn't even seen her. He had gone into a white-painted building which Jo had never noticed before.

Harbour Street Chapel,
Gospel Services 10.30a.m. and 6.30p.m.
God willing

said a sign.

So this was Jaz's church. Jo wondered idly what life was like with these religious freaks. Twice every Sunday seemed an awful chore. Jo knew Jaz was expected to go. She seemed quite normal, considering.

I suppose you know where you are with that sort of family, thought Jo, as she turned to cross the foot-bridge.

Back home there was a note on the galley table.

55

'Darling,

I've gone to a friend's house. Phone 0903 826991 in emergency. Pizza in the freezer. I'll be back for supper.

PS Dad phoned. He says he can't make it today, something came up. He sent his love. Love you too. Mum.'

'Blow 'em. Who cares?' Jo tumbled into bed, without even bothering to undress. Within seconds her mind was drifting into blissful nothingness.

It seemed as if she had only just sunk to the depths of sleep, when a noisy powerboat going up-river brought her struggling to the surface. The clock across the water chimed. She counted. Nine o'clock, or was it? Ten. Eleven.

Suddenly clear-headed, Jo considered what to do with the rest of the day. She wondered about Jaz. Why hadn't she said goodbye last night? Was she OK? There was nothing else to do, so Jo decided to go and find out.

She grabbed a chocolate bar and a bag of crisps and leapt on her bike. The Walcotts' house was empty, so she cycled on to the little chapel. It seemed silent until she got close enough to hear the distant drone of a sermon. Mildly curious, she crept up to the door.

'The devil has many ways of making his temptations seem attractive. And harmless, at first . . .' The door was slightly ajar and it was Pastor Walcott's voice she could hear through the gap. Jo's thoughts drifted back to Abby.

'What are you doing to change the world you live in? If you see something bad, are you just going to sit by and do nothing? God wants people like you to stand up and fight evil in the world. Don't tell me there's nothing you can do. God wants you!'

It seemed to Jo that this last remark was thundered straight at her. She glanced up alarmed to see if the door had somehow opened to reveal her. It hadn't. She could see him through the crack, but it was clear he couldn't see her. He dropped his voice to a dramatic plea. 'Say yes to God today. Let him speak to you. Take a risk and see what adventures he will lead you into.' A pause. 'Shall we bow our heads in prayer.'

Everything went quiet. Jo wasn't into this prayer lark. But fighting, yes. Nobody could say Jodi Thomas wasn't a fighter. She had never really thought much about evil before, but this morning it was real. It was a syringe in a bathroom cabinet.

Right, she thought. I'm not gonna sit back and let it happen. Abby, watch out.

She sat on the steps in a deep sun-warmed silence. 'OK God, you can speak to me, if you like,' she offered, but there was no thunderous voice from heaven, only an out-of-tune piano striking up the last hymn.

Eventually the singing stopped. Jo retreated across the road, just in case these gospel freaks could see at a glance that she needed converting. After a silence the door jerked open and a few people trickled out.

It was ages before Jaz came out. When she did, she was deep in conversation with a spotty, lanky youth. Suddenly awkward, Jo didn't know whether to interrupt, but Jaz spotted her and rushed across the road.

'Who's he?' demanded Jo.

'Oh, that's Barney. He's OK,' said Jaz dismissively. 'How late did it go on last night? Was it good?'

'Yeah, brilliant,' said Jo. 'I didn't go to bed till three o'clock. What happened to you? Did you enjoy it?'

'Yeah, great,' said Jaz. 'I looked for you, but I had to

go. Where were you?'

'I dunno. Perhaps it was when I was out on the fire escape. I was talking to this amazing bloke. Dimitri his name was. He's a poet.'

'Your sister knows some fantastic people. I thought you were meeting your dad today?'

'Oh yeah, I was, but something's come up. He's always busy. Got a gig with the band, I expect. That's usually why he can't make it.' (Well, sometimes it is, thought Jo to herself. I don't know about all the other times.)

'Why don't you come to lunch?' Jaz asked. 'Mum always cooks extra for Sunday lunch.'

'What for?' queried Jo.

'Oh, she likes hospitality. She says you can entertain angels unawares.'

The 'angels' at the Walcotts' dinner table this Sunday were Jo, Auntie Edie and Cousin Leroy from London, and old Mr Simkins who had been a pillar of the chapel for fifty years and was very deaf.

'He keeps going to sleep,' explained Jaz, 'and then wakes up and starts praying out loud at all the wrong times.'

The Walcotts were good with their unaware angels. They were the sort of people who made you feel at home the moment you arrived. It was impossible to feel an outsider with them.

'Jaz says your family are very artistic,' said Mrs Walcott. Jo agreed. Yes, her mum and her sister were both artists. Yes, her dad played in a band. 'No, I'm the odd one out, I'm not good at any of that stuff.'

Had Pastor Walcott noticed something in her voice? 'Talent isn't all that matters,' he remarked quietly.

58

'Character's far more important.'

Jo would have liked to ask him what character was, but just then baby Clifford spilt his plate of gravy over Mr Simkins and it was back to the usual Walcott mealtime uproar.

After lunch Jo was handed a tea-towel and Pastor Walcott put on an apron. Everyone was expected to pitch in and help with the washing-up. A preacher in a Desperate Dan apron seemed odd to Jo. 'His name's Daniel,' explained Jaz.

This was the moment for the family to analyse the sermon.

'Only four "finally"s today, Dad,' said Alex.

'And six "the fact of the matter"s,' said Jaz.

'Who was that lady in front of me?' asked Aunt Edie. 'She seemed a bit put out.'

'It was when you said about people who only care about appearances,' added Leroy.

'Oh dear. That's Mrs Aspen,' said Mum. 'She thinks you don't like her flower arrangements.'

'I only suggested she might make them a little lower,' said Pastor Walcott.

This remark reduced the entire family to helpless laughter. Jaz eventually recovered enough to explain that Pastor Walcott (who could hardly be described as tall) had preached his first sermon hidden behind a grand floral display that Mrs Aspen had over-enthusiastically attached to the pulpit.

'Like a pygmy in the jungle,' spluttered Alex.

'And he was talking about church growth,' added Mrs Walcott.

The Reverend didn't seem to mind at all. He gave as good as he got with a fair amount of mickey-taking and flicking around of washing-up water. It all ended with a full-scale bundle in the garden, involving everyone except Mr Simkins, who was snoring peacefully in an armchair.

It was a long time since Jo had been in a family which did things together. It seemed like fun.

6

A Trip Round the Pier

'I like your family,' said Jo to Jaz as they wandered along the beach later that afternoon.

'Yeah, it's OK, I guess,' agreed Jaz. 'A bit boring. Yours is far more interesting.'

Perhaps other people's families always seem better than your own. Jo pondered this theory silently for a while as they splashed through the foam. It was a good place for thinking, with your feet sinking in the soft sand and the tide draining away between your toes.

'What were you doing on the fire escape with this Dimitri?' demanded Jaz, puncturing her thoughts.

'Oh nothing, just talking. He was really interesting. What about that guy you were dancing with? He looked a bit of a dish.'

'Oh him. He wasn't as nice as he looked.' It was Jaz's turn to be vague. The thought of the way he'd tried to touch her made her shudder. But perhaps older girls liked that sort of thing.

'Your sister's cool. I liked her flat.' Jo was so familiar with it that she rarely noticed the posters and ornamental fans on the wall, the junk shop bric-à-brac and the cushions on the floor.

'Yeah...' She was almost tempted to share her worries about Abby, but just then her thoughts were disturbed by a Range Rover towing a small boat and roaring over the beach towards them.

'Mind out!' yelled a voice, and the vehicle squealed to a halt at the water's edge, spraying them with sand and water. The guy at the wheel looked familiar. It was the jogger from *Shangri-La*.

'Idiot,' muttered Jo, but Jaz's shy 'Hello' had an air of reverent admiration.

'Oh, hi girls,' said the blond, bronzed figure, with a vague air of recognition. 'The spies, isn't it?'

He leapt out of the car. 'You couldn't do me a favour, could you? Help me launch the boat.'

'Yes, of course,' Jaz agreed eagerly. Jo was just as keen but stayed cool. 'OK, if it doesn't take long,' she agreed.

First the trailer had to be taken into the wavelets, and the boat pushed off. Jaz quickly saw what needed doing and rushed to help. Jo followed and together they slid the boat into the sea.

'Now, if you could just keep an eye on it for me, while I drive the trailer back up to the road...' and he was gone, leaving them knee-deep in water, icy still in late May.

They watched him drive up the beach and disappear over the top. There was a long pause. Clouds scudded across the sky, dogs barked and children shrieked in the distance. The blond boatman didn't reappear. 'If he doesn't come back soon, I think we ought to let it float out to sea,' said Jo, with no real intention of doing so. She was far too curious about the boat's owner.

Eventually, just as their toes were getting numb, he

returned, jumping down gracefully over the shingle.

'Thanks, girls. That was really good of you. You're a godsend, you know. I was supposed to have a couple of girlfriends helping me, but they didn't show up. What a stroke of luck, eh?'

'Aren't you gonna give us a ride then?' Jo asked boldly. Jaz looked at her in astonishment.

The jogger laughed. 'Yes, why not? I'm only taking her for a little spin. I've got to go down to the Marina to collect something, then back round into the river to moor her. Hop aboard.'

Jaz hesitated. 'Never go with strangers,' had been drummed into her for at least the last ten years.

'It's all right,' hissed Jo. 'There's two of us. And he's a neighbour. We know where he lives. You can swim, can't ya?'

'Yes.'

'So if he tries anything, we'll jump out and swim for it.'

'Well then?' he asked, as the waves crashed and the sea sparkled around him.

'You bet.' Jo and Jaz scrambled aboard. With a run he pushed the little boat out, jumped in and switched the motor into life.

'Perhaps we ought to introduce ourselves,' he yelled over the engine's roar. 'My name's Sebastian. Sebastian Raphael.'

'I'm Jo Thomas,' bawled Jo. Jaz had to have three goes at communicating her name loudly enough.

They raced out well beyond the breakers, before he turned towards Brighton and settled the engine to a steady chug.

'Nothing like it, is there, being at sea?'

'It's lovely,' agreed Jaz, who had never been at sea before.

Jo breathed deeply and licked the salt from her lips. 'Is it your hobby?'

'More of a passion really—boats. That's why I came back here. River and sea—and the airfield. What could be better? Put to sea when you want to, go flying if you feel like it. Either way you're taking off into the blue. You need that after the city.'

'Have you got a plane too?'

'Not quite, but I've got my pilot's licence. I can hire one if I want to.'

'Must be bloomin' expensive.'

'Bloomin' expensive,' he agreed. 'But I work hard for my money, and there's only me to spend it on. No point if you can't indulge yourself a little.'

'So what d'you do the rest of the time? You said you travelled,' reminded Jo.

'Did I? Oh yes. Well, it just depends what business projects I've got on at the time. Right now I've decided to have a break for a while.'

'What kind of projects?' Jo was curious.

'Oh, promotions. Concerts, exhibitions, shows, organizing tours.'

'Have you done rock concerts?'

'Quite a few. Wembley, NEC, Hammersmith Odeon. Big names, mostly.'

'What, Prince, U2, that sorta thing?'

'That sort of thing,' Sebastian agreed.

Jo and Jaz gazed at him in dumbstruck awe.

'It's an artificial life, though,' he continued. 'That's why I like to get back to basics. A bit of hard work. Scrubbing decks, hoisting sails. Man against the sea—

alone in the ocean. Elemental stuff.'

The pause as they pondered this simple life was broken by an electronic bleeping. From a bag they hadn't noticed, stashed under the seat, Sebastian drew a cellphone. One hand on the wheel, he pitted himself, not just against the elements, but against an unseen business client, who, judging by this end of the conversation, was less than satisfied.

'What else do you expect for that price? I got it to you on time, didn't I? You won't get a better offer from anyone else.'

Figures were muttered. They were all expressed in 'grands'.

'That's thousands,' explained Jo in an undertone to Jaz. At one point half a million was mentioned. The girls were impressed.

Sebastian was less happy. 'If you don't like it, you can go elsewhere. I don't need your business. You're small fry to me.'

He drew in the phone's aerial and slammed it down. For a moment his businessman's cool dropped away. He was rattled.

They had passed the stone pier at the end of the long tongue of land that was Shoreham Beach, and were level with the lighthouse which marked the river's passage into the sea. Tidy bungalows gave way to derelict warehouses. The tall landmark chimney loomed into view. From here you could see that the power station it served had long since been demolished.

The carefree atmosphere was gone. Sebastian stared thunderously ahead and muttered a few of the words that Pastor Walcott wouldn't allow in the house.

Then abruptly the storm passed and he flashed them his butter-melting smile. 'Sorry about that. Just a bit of business. Let's step on it.'

He turned the engine on full, and the boat was soaring bumpily over the surface of the sea. 'Day trip round the pier,' he yelled. The girls held on tight as warehouses and boatyards gave way to genteel hotels. Deckchairs and windbreaks dotted the beaches and they could hear children squealing as they jumped the waves.

They were racing towards Brighton and the West Pier rose before them. From a distance, it looked like a silvered fairy-tale palace, a mysterious island on stilts. Close-to, the fantasy resolved into dereliction and decay. The pier had been cut off from land since the fire that sealed its doom. It had been left to rot in splendid isolation.

On they plunged towards the gloomy underside of the burnt-out pier. Beyond it a few other boats could be seen. Sailing dinghies, darting windsurfers, and a motor launch with some uniformed men aboard.

Sebastian pulled into sudden reverse and they slowed to a standstill amid the rusting pillars.

I wonder if anyone from the shore can see us here, thought Jaz. Suppose he murders us and pushes us overboard?

But he merely said, 'Sorry, girls. Change of plan. Time I was going back,' and he circled the boat in a wide arc round the pier and headed for home.

This time they went in at the river mouth. They passed a few container ships and smaller tankers—none of them grand or exciting. Beyond the run-down docks, they were coming back to Jo's part of the river.

The footbridge was silhouetted before them in the afternoon sun. But, before they reached it, Sebastian was turning the boat into the quayside.

'This is it. Let me introduce you to *Peggy Sue*.'

Peggy Sue was an old wooden fishing boat. She was in the mid-stages of getting shipshape, and you could see how a lick of paint would bring out her charm.

Day trips to France.
Night-time mackerel fishing.
Charter boat for hire with crew

said a notice.

'My latest venture. More for the fun than the money. I'm the crew, when I feel like it,' said Sebastian. 'When I don't, I hire in. There's plenty of people around here can sail a boat like this for a bit of extra cash.'

'It's lovely,' said Jaz.

'She, please,' said Sebastian. 'Boats are always "she".'

He was tying up the little motor boat next to *Peggy Sue*.

'That's sexist,' grumbled Jo. 'Why can't you call a boat Fred or Harry?'

Sebastian laughed. 'You're quite right, but I rather like to think of my boat as "she". I suppose I just like female company.' He flashed them a smile. 'And I've enjoyed yours. But really I've got work to do.'

He offered them a gentlemanly hand as they scrambled up on to *Peggy Sue*.

'If you ever want crew members, I'm sure we could learn ever so quickly,' offered Jo hopefully.

'Thanks, I'll bear it in mind.'

'I'm at *Trade Winds*. It's just down the path from you.'

But from the depths of the little power boat came the bleep of the cellphone. Sebastian turned back to answer it, and Jo and Jaz stepped off on to dry land.

They found themselves on a narrow strip of quayside by a dusty scrapyard. The only way out was a door in a high wall. As they let themselves out, Sebastian was arguing into his phone. 'You'll just have to wait. I don't get paid till the end of the run,' they heard him say as the door shut behind them. They found themselves alongside the roar of traffic in the busy road.

The town they knew so well looked quite different from the river, like a familiar view in a looking-glass, and they paused, confused, until the unfamiliar street became one that Jaz at least knew very well.

They had come out not far from the little chapel and the thought of it made Jaz instinctively check her watch. 'Oh no, 6.08. Must dash. Mum'll kill me if I turn up at church like this.'

Jaz sped off home to change and Jo trudged slowly up the road behind her. The chapel, she noticed, was already open. She crossed the road and peered in. A fat man in a shiny suit was putting hymn books on pews, but he didn't see her. It was the smell Jo noticed. It was probably a mixture of furniture polish, damp walls and flower arrangements, but Jo couldn't identify it. To her it just smelt old. Not old, dead and musty like the parish church, not old and decaying like the pier, but old like something that had lived a long time and would live a long time yet.

Jo had only a hazy idea of the things the people of the old chapel believed in. 'The Lord's my shepherd.' 'Forgive us our trespasses.' Did it tie you down or make you feel safe? Jo wasn't sure.

She shrugged her shoulders and turned her mind to the more exciting events of the weekend. The party was becoming less scary in memory. So what if Abby experimented with a few drugs? That was what Abby was like—daring, always prepared to take risks.

She thought about Sebastian. What a great life. Live in a glamorous pop world when you want to. Put out to sea when you get tired of it.

No, the chapel folk were missing a lot, she decided, as she swung onto the footbridge and headed for home.

7

Dealings with Deceit

'My ring's missing,' said Mum. 'The one Auntie Ethel left me.'

'Oh Mum, come on. You know what you're like. I bet you've just forgotten where you put it . . .'

Jo stared across the table, open-mouthed, as Abby continued, ' . . . you know you're not the tidiest person in the world.'

Mum remained puzzled. 'I could have sworn it was in the mustard pot with the earrings. But you're right. You'd think in a place this size you couldn't lose things, but I manage it.'

She strained spaghetti over the sink. 'There's that all-singing, all-dancing camera your father gave me. I can't find that either. To be honest I was going to flog it. I'm never going to use the flippin' thing, and there's just too many red bills.'

Mum joined them at the table with the plates of steaming pasta. 'And I'm sorry to go on about it, Abby, but that two hundred quid. You said it was just till you got a new cashcard.'

'Oh, Mum, come on. It's the end of term. I'll get a holiday job.'

'Yeah, I know, I don't like nagging.'

'Cor, you nag me enough,' said Jo, but her heart wasn't in a sparring match right now.

Neither was Mum's. 'I don't know where the money goes. There's just never enough. I could have sworn I still had two twenties in my purse, but there's only a fiver left.'

Yes, thought Jo, and I *know* I had £17.50 in my pink pig a couple of weeks ago, and that's gone too.

But Abby just smiled and commiserated and made promises about all the things she'd buy Mum when she was a famous designer.

'That's all very well, but we have to eat now. Especially you. You look like you haven't had a decent meal in weeks.'

So Abby said nice things about Mum's cooking and pushed the food round her plate. And Jo ate her pasta and watched with narrowing eyes, while Mum told *her* she ought to be watching her weight.

After lunch, when Mum had retired with the Sunday papers, Jo and Abby sprawled on the patch of deck between the mop and bucket and the lifebelt. Jo wished it was just like any other Sunday. But it wasn't. Abby was pale and restless. She'd said she had a cold when Mum complained she'd hardly touched her food. She was moving edgily now, waiting for the earliest moment she could decently depart.

Jo knew she couldn't put it off. If she was going to fight evil, she'd have to do it now.

'Look, Abby, about these drugs.'

'What drugs?' Abby started defensively.

'You're taking drugs. I can tell. I'm not that daft.

71

Anyway, I found a syringe and some needles in your bathroom cabinet.'

'Who said you could nose around my flat?'

'I didn't do it on purpose.'

'Well, you shouldn't jump to conclusions. I wouldn't inject. I'm not that stupid. I was looking after them for a friend.'

'Like you're looking after Mum's ring?'

'You won't tell her, will you?' Abby's voice rose.

'Keep your voice down or she'll hear anyway. Not if you give it back.'

'Course I will.' But Abby hardly looked convincing.

'Anyway, it's not just the ring. And it isn't just the syringe. I saw you sniffing that powder.'

'Look, it's no problem. Promise me you won't tell Mum.' Abby kept her voice at a low mutter, but Jo could hear the panic.

'Why should I?'

'It was just to see me through the exams. I'm not addicted or anything. As soon as I've got all my projects done and things calm down, I won't need it. I'll pay her back. You don't know what it's like. And anyway, everyone else does it.'

'I don't care what anyone else does. You're my sister.'

'Promise you won't tell her? Please.'

'OK. Promise. But I still think you're being really stupid.'

Abby got up angrily. 'When I need you to tell me what to do, I'll ask. You're just a kid. And don't forget I've seen you smoking down on the rec and forging notes to school. You mind your own business and I'll mind mine. At least I've got something I'm good at. I've worked hard to get through college and I'm one of their best students. What have you ever done? You'll be lucky if you end up stacking shelves in Tesco's.'

She turned to go. 'Tell Mum I had things to do.'

Jo watched her all the way along the path until all she could see was her bobbing head going over the bridge. 'Well thanks, God, you were a great help there,' she muttered.

Fighting evil was definitely someone else's job, thought Jo. God might be on Jaz's side but he didn't seem to be on hers. Anyway, perhaps Abby was right and it really wasn't a problem . . .

Jo tried to forget about her conversation with Abby, and managed quite well until about three weeks later.

The week began with one of those rainy Mondays when everyone gets irritable with everyone else.

When Jaz had announced she was going to the Gym Club at lunchtime Jo had been cross. 'Don't you want to hang round with me then?'

'Yeah, but I like gym. There's not much else I'm good at in school and I've only just dared to put my name down. You can come too.'

So here they were in the gym with the rain pummelling on the windows and all the hearty athletic types, the ones Jo couldn't stand, hanging around the wall bars.

They stared at Jaz and Jo, and Jo stared back.

Miss Davies bustled in. 'Ah, Jasmine Walcott. Glad you could join us. I've heard good reports of you from class . . . Well, Jodi Thomas, to what do we owe the honour?' (Jo was well-known for skipping PE lessons.)

'I've decided gymnastics is interesting, Miss.'

'So perhaps you could get changed into your gym kit.'

'Er, no, Miss, I've got a bad leg at the moment and my Mum says I shouldn't risk it.'

Miss Davies sighed. 'Well, just stand in the corner and keep out of the way of the others. Now Jasmine, perhaps you could give us a short mat routine, to show what you can do.'

Jaz ran gracefully to the centre of the mat and back-flipped effortlessly. The other girls stopped their exercises and turned to look. Jo had no idea of the names of the somersaults and movements that Jaz was doing, but she was impressed. So, it seemed, was everyone else. There was even a smattering of applause when Jaz finished with the splits, holding the pose as easily as if she was sitting in an armchair. This was something else Jo didn't know about her friend.

'Well Jasmine, you have been hiding your light under a bushel. Where did you learn this?'

'At my old school, Miss Davies, and at dance classes.'

'Very good indeed. I could use you in our team for the East Sussex display. See me afterwards, will you? Now everyone, we're going to do some work on the parallel bars . . .'

After the practice Miss Davies called Jaz over and they seemed to have quite a long, complicated discussion. Jo hung around for Jaz to come out of the changing rooms, but when she did she was surrounded by other girls.

'You'll be the star of the team.'

'Can you teach me your running cartwheel?'

'That double somersault was brilliant.'

Jo sloped off to CDT in disgust.

After school it was just as bad. Those snobby Sarahs

and Fionas who had looked down their noses at Jaz when she first arrived were all over her now.

Jo followed grumpily behind, listening in to the conversation.

'So what does old Davey want you to do in the display?'

'It's a real honour. She usually only chooses people who've been around for donkey's years.'

'We'll come and cheer you on.'

Jaz stopped. 'Actually,' she said quietly, 'I'm not sure I will be in it. It's on a Sunday, you see.'

The other girls crowded round her.

'So?'

'Why not?'

'What's the difference?'

'Well, I go to church on Sunday mornings.'

'Oh no, a religious nut.'

'Surely you could miss it just once?'

'You'd be mad not to.'

'You'd let the club down.'

'Miss Davies would never give you another chance.'

Jo, standing behind Jaz, noticed her friend's chin quiver just a little. That was it.

She barged in. 'Look, if she doesn't want to, that's her business.'

'Didn't know you were into gymnastics, Jodi.'

'Or religion.'

'Why not? What's wrong with religion? Better than soppy old gymnastics anyway. Just leave her alone.'

The other girls went off laughing.

'Jodi Thomas's got religion.'

'Hallelujah, praise de Lord.'

Their laughter echoed down the corridor.

'Thanks,' said Jaz, as they took the plunge into the grey rainy playground. 'I could have stood up for myself, you know.'

'Yeah, course. But they're real bitchy when they get going. Believe me, I know. You're not really gonna chuck up the gym display for church, are you? You can go to church any time.'

'I don't know.' Jaz looked worried.

'But why? Won't your parents let you do it?'

'No, they wouldn't stop me. It's just something I think I ought to do,' explained Jaz hesitantly. 'It's about, sort of, um, putting God first. I'll have to pray about it.' She leapt an extra big puddle. 'I'm glad you think religion's OK, though. I thought you thought it was a bit silly.'

'Nah, it's all right, if you like that sort of thing,' said Jo, splashing her way through the puddles. What she thought was, 'Pray about it. Good grief!'

All week Jaz went around looking troubled and Jo heard on the grapevine that she had refused to do the display. It was not until Thursday that Jaz came bounding up to her with a great big grin. 'Guess what! I'm going to do the gym display.'

'Great, did you give up on this church stuff?'

'No, we're not on till the afternoon.'

'Did old Davey get the time wrong?'

'No, they changed it at the last minute.'

'Lucky.'

Jaz looked indignant. 'Lucky! That wasn't just lucky. That was an answered prayer.'

On the way home Jo puzzled about answered prayer. It was rubbish ... wishful thinking ... just a coincidence. Or was it? She remembered Pastor Walcott and his talk of fighting evil. He seemed to think praying had something to do with that. Perhaps that was what she got wrong.

Well, why not? thought Jo. Nothing else seems to be working. She screwed up her eyes, not quite closing them because that seemed a bit dangerous on a bike.

'OK, if you are there, God, and I'm not too sure that you are, and even if you are, I don't suppose I'm the type you answer—but anyway, please help me get Abby off drugs. You do something. I don't know what. Amen.'

The next day Jo bunked off from double science, not an unusual event. It was Mum's day for pottery, so she was surprised to hear voices when she arrived back at *Trade Winds* in the middle of the day. She peered down the hatchway into the cabin. She could hear Abby and a voice she didn't recognize. She could see someone else, a youngish guy who looked vaguely familiar.

'Look, you promised you'd get me some,' said Abby. 'I've got the money. What's the problem?'

'He won't be there yet. He said he'd be home at three o'clock. Don't get so uptight. Anyone would think you were hooked or something.' He laughed a cold, scornful laugh and Jo remembered where she'd heard it before. It was at Abby's party and he was the guy who'd been passing round the white powder.

She shrank back from the hatchway, thought for a moment and then clattered obviously down the steps.

Abby jumped. 'Oh hi, it's you. Bunking school again. This is my sister.'

'Hi,' said Jo and gave the guy a hard stare.

'Oh, this is Mick. A friend of mine. I've finished lectures, so we thought we'd come over.'

There was an uncomfortable silence.

'It's five to three,' said Abby.

'Yeah, well, I'd better be off,' said Mick. 'I'll get the stuff and come right back.'

'What stuff's that?' asked Jo with as much innocence as she could muster.

'Art supplies. Just art supplies,' said Mick and pushed past her out of the cabin.

Left together in the cabin, the silence continued. Abby avoided Jo's eyes and stared out of the porthole. She shifted uncomfortably from side to side and picked at her nails. They were bitten, Jo noticed. Abby's nails had always been long and beautiful.

Jo busied herself in the galley. 'Wanna cup of tea?' she managed.

'Yeah, ta.'

They drank their tea in silence, but it was soon broken by Mick's return. He seemed triumphant.

'There. Told you I wouldn't be long.'

'You got some?' Abby muttered.

'Yeah, plenty. Fresh in. I told you he's a useful guy to know. How much, then?'

'Not here.' Abby got up and propelled him out. 'Bye, kid. See you.'

'Bye,' said Jo casually and listened for their footsteps to get over the gangplank before she came up to the hatchway and watched.

Mick was handing Abby some small packets. She was giving him some money as they went off laughing.

Numb and angry, Jo stared at their retreating

figures. Her eyes pricked with tears. Blindly she stumbled back into the cabin and sat huddled in Mum's rocking chair, trying to make sense of what she had seen. If ever she had convinced herself that drugs were just a phase Abby was going through, she couldn't believe it now. She pictured Abby's white face and urgent, shaking hands and knew otherwise. This wasn't something you could just shake free of.

Tears dropped on the cushion as she puzzled what to do.

Tell Mum? She thought of her mother, sometimes bright and funny, sometimes uptight and weepy. She tried so hard to do all the good-mum things, but sometimes you could see she was struggling underneath. And anyway, she had promised Abby. She wouldn't tell Mum. Not yet anyway.

Tell Dad? Chance would be a fine thing.

Who else? She couldn't think.

And what about Mick? Yes, what about Mick? She remembered his slight, weasel-like figure and his sneering smile. She thumped the cushion in blind fury.

He wasn't getting away with this. He was the one pushing the drugs. Get rid of him and the problem might be solved. She stood up and brushed away the tears. That was it. She was going to the police.

Leaping on her bike and pedalling over the bridge with the cool wind on her face made her feel better. It also made her think a bit more clearly. Just what could she tell the police? There was someone called Mick, who she thought lived in Brighton somewhere, and ... Well, that was their problem. They were supposed to be good at that sort of thing.

She was just coming to the end of the footbridge when she looked up and saw Mick right ahead of her. She came to an abrupt halt behind him, but the squeal of the brakes made him turn. He gave her a suspicious look. 'Hi,' she said weakly, stalling for time to think, but he turned and continued up the High Street. Where was he going? Off to a new customer? Back to the supplier? She scanned the faces around her. Abby was nowhere to be seen.

Suddenly he turned again. 'You following me?' he demanded.

Jo faced him, her fury boiling over. 'As it happens, no, I ain't. I'm goin' to the police station. And when I get there I'm goin' to report you for pushing drugs. What do you think you're doin'? Getting at people when they're down. Making money out of their stupidity. Watching them get worse and worse while you rake in the profit!'

He went as if to hit her. She flinched, putting the bike between them. People turned to stare.

'Listen,' he hissed. 'If you want to tell the police about me, go ahead. I can tell them a thing or two about your sister. Where do you think she gets her money from? It doesn't all come from your mum's purse. She's been nicking from college funds. Don't look so shocked. It's true, I can prove it.

'And don't think she's above selling the stuff herself, either. We're in the same boat, her and me. Why do you think I push it? So, shop me and they get her too. If I go down, she sinks with me.'

He turned away and made off down the High Street, striding defiantly for a few paces before breaking into a run.

Jo stood, gripping her bike. Her knuckles were white, but she knew if she released them she would start to shake. Mick was scared too, she realized that. His threats came out of blind panic. But she had no doubt he would fulfil them, and she had a horrible feeling that what he was saying was true.

Slowly she headed back for home. Pedalling wearily along the footpath she saw the weird boy, Gary, wandering round his little patch of garden. He stared blankly as she passed. She grinned ruefully. It was only a few weeks ago they had played detective, looking for the drugs smuggler. It had seemed like a game then.

It was then that the thought struck her. It was obvious. And she'd totally overlooked it. Wherever Mick had got his 'supplies', it could hardly be far away. He'd been gone barely ten minutes.

Someone, somewhere very near, was dealing out the white powder that was turning her sister into a junkie, a thief and a liar. And whoever it was lived no more than five minutes away from *Trade Winds*!

8

Only Connect

Even if Jo did want to fight evil, it seemed she was not much good at it. Just forget it, she told herself. But however much she tried, she couldn't.

Every time she left home she would stare at the houses and houseboats she passed, searching their blank frontages in vain for clues. Everyone she passed became a suspicious character, or at least every man, because she remembered clearly that Mick had said 'he'.

Every time she switched on TV there seemed to be a desperate, haunted addict somewhere in the story. And each time Abby paid her shorter, tenser and less frequent visits home, she looked to Jo's searching eyes more hollow and jittery.

Jo hadn't confided her worries about Abby to Jaz and somehow in the last few weeks she and Jaz had drifted apart.

After her brief dealings with God, Jo had decided that even if she was prepared to be on speaking terms with him, he wasn't too interested in her. She came to the conclusion that this religious stuff was a load of old rubbish. Even if it worked for some people, it certainly wasn't working for her. She told Jaz so in no uncertain terms and Jaz retired hurt—thinking, wrongly, that if Jo didn't like what she believed, she didn't like her.

Jo in her turn interpreted her friend's distance with, 'I'm not good enough for her because I don't believe that stuff.'

And there was another reason why Jo decided she wasn't good enough. Jaz took home a gold medal from the East Sussex display and overnight became a school star.

The Head, who made a fuss when someone from Downview came top in anything, announced that here was excellence everyone should copy. Girls who had described Jaz as 'that boring religious kid', now decided to be her friend. She got invitations to tea with the sort of girls who had ponies and ballet lessons. She felt uneasy in their grand homes and longed for a giggle and a bag of chips with someone more ordinary, but somehow felt she couldn't admit it.

By now Mrs Walcott had got into the local grapevine and discovered that Jodi Thomas was known as a 'bad influence'. She tried not to interfere, but her pleasure at Jaz's new 'nice' friends, and her worries about Jo, got across all too clearly.

To make matters worse, it was exam time and Jo decided that since she hadn't worked all year, it was pointless taking the exams. Her absences began to be commented on, and she was seen smoking in alleyways. (I can give it up any time I want to, she told herself.)

The Head contacted Maggie Thomas, and Maggie came home and threw a wobbler at Jo. It ended with Maggie bursting into tears and the 'Where did I go wrong? How can I be expected to bring two girls up on my own?' routine.

Jo found the tears a lot worse than the lecture, but she wasn't letting on that either of them had any effect.

However, they did have one consequence. Dad actually turned up for one of his weekend visits—and spent it telling Jo what a disappointment she was and how he expected a daughter of his to do better.

Abby just said, 'Decided to be a drop-out, have you?', and impressed Mum and Dad by inviting them to her end-of-year display of work. Jo tagged along, seething, but had to admit that the costumes Abby had designed and made up were breathtakingly beautiful. She peered at them closely. Was it just her imagination, or were those done at the end of the year less neat and detailed than those at the beginning?

Under pressure, Jo went back to school for the end of term. It was pointless because all they had were videos and quizzes and the incredibly boring Sports Day. One afternoon the entire lower school were shunted into the hall for a talk on 'Harmful Substances: Addiction and Abuse'.

'Jodi Thomas smokes,' said Masher Barnes when nicotine was under discussion. Jo delved in her pencil case for her compasses and poked him hard in the leg. The speaker, a trainee doctor wishing desperately he was back in the Health Centre, pretended he hadn't heard either the comment or the yelp of pain which followed it.

Coming out of the hall, Jo bumped into Jaz. There was no avoiding each other and Jaz smiled hopefully. Jo offered a grin and they walked the corridor side by side in silence.

'You did good in gym, then,' Jo said eventually.

'Yes,' said Jaz. There was a pause while she tried to think of something Jo had done good.

'Still hallelujahing?' asked Jo.

'I still go to church, if that's what you mean,' said Jaz defensively.

'Right, good, that's good,' said Jo. 'All this gym stuff fit in, then?'

'Yes, it's been Saturdays mostly. I've been quite busy.'

'Thought you had.'

Jo fished in her bag. 'Here, have a substance.'

Jaz looked worried until she saw the substance on offer was a bag of wine gums.

They sucked in silence as they swung out of the school gates.

'You don't really smoke, do you?' Jaz asked after a while.

'Nah—well, just the odd one or two. I'm not hooked or anything.'

'No, I didn't think you would be ... I don't know why they tell us all that stuff. People round here aren't into all those hard drugs.'

Jo went quiet.

'Anyone who is must be really stupid, I think,' continued Jaz. 'People who do drugs must have really empty lives.'

'What d'you know about it? They might just be stressed or something. They could be really clever. A lot are.'

Jaz glanced round in surprise. Jo's voice had risen defiantly. 'Yes, well, I expect you're right. You probably know more about these sorts of things than I do.'

'Why should I? Why d'you say that?'

'Don't get uptight with me,' protested Jaz, puzzled. 'I just meant that everyone knows more about life than me.'

Jo muttered something and turned her head away. Jaz could have sworn she saw a tear in her eye. She decided on diversion tactics. 'Anyway, I'm addicted to wine gums. Got any more?'

For all her shyness, Jaz had a way of putting people at ease. She told Jo about the latest gym display and how the minibus had left Lewes without Miss Davies and no one had mentioned it until they got back to school.

By the time they reached the footbridge they were chatting away like old friends once more.

'D'you wanna come over to the Beach?' Jo asked.

'Better not, I promised Mum I'd look after Clifford while she went to Asda. Tell you what, I said I'd take old Mr Simkins' dog for a walk after tea. Why don't you come? I've found this lovely path up to the Downs.'

Whenever Dad wanted to take her on country walks, Jo refused point-blank. But two hours later, with Blackie snuffling and straining on the leash, they were heading up through the fields with the traffic only a distant hum below.

They climbed steadily until they were almost at the top. Looking back, they could see the river snaking its way down to the town. On the airfield beside it, light aircraft were taking off and landing like orderly insects. Little white dots played cricket on the rec. Far beyond, the sea gleamed in the evening sun. Even the seagulls were circling below them.

They threw themselves on the spongy grass, sprawling lazily in the golden light. Lost in the clear blue above their heads, an unknown bird was trilling a song. It was good to be friends with Jaz again, thought Jo. And there was six weeks' holiday, starting the day after tomorrow. Perhaps things were beginning to look up.

Jo wondered why she'd never been on the Downs before. Things looked different from up here.

Suddenly she sat up. 'Look, you can even see *Trade Winds*.'

Jaz stared. 'Where?'

'See the bridge? Look straight across from there at the boat with the really tall mast. Count six along from that.'

Jaz screwed up her eyes. 'Oh yes. You can even see people on the path. Look, I bet that's that horrible man—the one we thought was a smuggler. Weren't we daft about that?'

'No, not really. There is someone shifting drugs down there, I know for a fact. And he's only five minutes away from *Trade Winds*.'

'How do you know?'

'Oh, I just know. That's all.'

A dark suspicion passed over Jaz's mind like a cloud over the sunny landscape.

'Look, if you're ever tempted—I mean, I know you find life hard sometimes, school and your dad an' all—don't give in. I'll pray for you, and I know you think Christians are silly and everything, but it could help and . . .'

'I don't need your Jesus stuff. I'm fine. Well, OK, anyway.'

'You can tell me, honest. I wouldn't split on you.'

'What? Oh, I get it . . . Look, what'ya take me for? I'm not that stupid. I wouldn't do drugs if you paid me.'

'Yes, but . . .'

'It's not me!'

Jo's voice dropped. 'It's not me. It's Abby.'

There, it was out, and Jo felt an enormous relief. Finally she could tell someone. The words tumbled out. About how no one else had noticed, about the syringe, about Mick going out and coming back with the white packets and what he'd said about Abby. About the arguments, the stealing, about Abby getting paler and thinner and the marks she'd seen on her arms last time she came.

Jaz was horrifed, but relieved too. She really had begun to wonder about Jo. 'Look, why don't we get her to talk to someone?'

'You're joking. She wouldn't even admit it to me.'

Jaz stared at the sea and thought. 'Well, what about the dealer? We know he's no more than five minutes from your boat. We could watch each house in turn.'

'I've been watching them, believe me. And do you know how many places there are within five minutes? Seventy-nine. I've counted.'

'Why don't we just tell the police what we know and let them sort it out?'

'Because we don't know anything definite.'

'We know Mick's pushing drugs and we know he's getting them from somewhere on the Beach.'

Jo heaved a sigh. 'Yeah, and we know Abby's taking them and stealing to do it. She's my sister, I don't want her in jail.'

'We needn't mention her.'

'Yeah, but someone else will.' Jo didn't trust Mick.

Jaz had no answer. Somewhere above the rec a kite fluttered. She stared idly as it swooped and turned. Someone must be controlling it, but it was impossible to see the string. She could make out a boy standing alone in the green field. It must be him, but she couldn't quite make the connection.

'That's it! ... This Mick, do you know where he lives?'

'Brighton somewhere. He hangs about the college ... 'cept term's finished now. He's got a funny name. Valentino or something.'

'Well, then. That's what we need to do. Follow him and see where he leads us. We just need to make the connection.'

9

Café Society

'But what if he recognizes me?'

'He won't.' Jaz glanced at the apparition on the seat next to her and giggled.

Jo was certainly not looking herself today. Hidden behind Mum's floppy velvet hat and a big pair of sunglasses, she had dressed herself all in black and given herself some bright red lipstick to complete the transformation.

Jaz wondered if they had overdone it. Here on the top of the bus to Brighton, they looked a bit over-dressed and conspicuous. The bus was full of brightly-coloured holiday makers. So were the beaches, the prom, the crazy golf. The sun was like a magnet, drawing them towards the sea.

'Where is this Arches Café anyway?'

'It's sort of under the prom, down by the pier.'

'And you're sure Abby won't be there?'

'Nah. She hardly ever goes out these days.'

'So she's still on drugs?'

The woman in front turned to look.

'Keep your voice down,' hissed Jo. 'I don't want to discuss Abby with the whole bus.'

She didn't really want to discuss her at all. It was too painful. But she knew Jaz's persistence. 'I went over there the other day,' she admitted, 'and she was stoned out of her mind. Wouldn't hardly speak to me. She's not designing or sewing or sculpting or anything.'

'But it's the end of term.'

'Yeah, I suppose. But she's not going off anywhere. Last year it was grape-picking in Israel. The year before it was helping at a kids' camp in Ohio. Now she's just sitting there looking blank. It's not like her.'

Jo's voice tailed off and she turned away. Jaz tried to cheer her. 'Anyway, you did find out about Mick.'

For a moment Jo brightened. 'Yeah. Clever huh? It's his dad's café. He helps out when it's busy.'

It would surely be busy today. Jo stared down at the crowded prom. All these people out enjoying themselves. The scene turned into a brightly-coloured blur. She fumbled for a tissue. 'It's the wind, something in my eyes.'

There was a silence.

'This pier?'

They were just approaching the derelict West Pier. Windsurfers darted over the glittering water like crazed butterflies.

'No, the next one.'

Jaz tried to change the subject. 'I saw Sebastian the other day.'

They giggled at the name, and rolled their eyes at the thought of the bronzed jogger.

'On his boat?'

'No, at the station all dressed in a suit. He was flying off for a few days, he said.'

'I wonder what he does.'

'He told us, promotions. He was booking some gigs in the States.'

'He might know about being a dancer. You ought to ask him.'

Jaz thought about being a dancer. About flying off to the States for a few days. About people who sat around doing nothing because of drugs. What a lot of different ways to spend your life.

Jo interrupted her thoughts. 'Come on, we're here.'

They clattered down the stairs and leapt off. Jo darted through the traffic, pulling Jaz with her. They dived under the rusty cast-iron arches that supported the upper promenade. 'When we get there, act cool. It's a trendy place.' They hustled past candy-floss shops, fish and chip shops, Brighton rock shops, postcard stands, and tubs full of fishing nets, flip-flops and kiss-me-quick hats. It seemed that when people got to Brighton they couldn't think of anything else to do except spend money.

The Arches Café certainly followed some sort of trend. You could tell it a mile off by the row of motor bikes outside and the heavy thump of music. They peered in the windows, eyes adjusting to the gloom. Dark figures sat motionless round black plastic tables.

'That's him, behind the counter.'

Mick turned round towards the windows and they backed off hastily.

'I . . . I'm not sure I want to go in there on my own,' said Jaz, quickly turning to the postcard stand outside the shop next door.

'That's not fair. It was your idea.'

'Yes, but . . .'

The café door opened. A group of hefty bikers came

out. Jaz peered out from behind the postcards and saw armfuls of tattoos, but Jo had caught a glimpse inside the door. 'Listen, there's a table right in the corner. I'll sit with my back to the counter, but you'll have to keep watch. Come on.'

Jo dragged the hat down over her eyes, and pulled Jaz in. She made for the corner table with her head turned towards the wall.

'You can order. Mine's a coke.'

Jaz and Jo sipped their cokes in uneasy silence. They had no clear plan of campaign. They had found Mick, but now what? They had timed their visit for half past four. 'It probably closes at five,' Jaz had suggested. 'Then we can follow him.'

But the sign on the wall said it closed at 9 p.m. 'We can't sit here until nine,' thought Jo. Jaz was feeling very uncomfortable sitting there at all. One or two girls hung around the juke-box, but most of the tables were taken up by big guys in leathers. 'At least we got the black gear right,' she thought. But there they sat, neither wishing to admit to the other that they were wasting time. Jaz watched the counter with determination, but Mick just went on making coffees and burgers. Jo stared, fascinated, at the painted and studded leather. Iron Maiden, skulls, wizards and swastikas stared back at her. 'One day I'll have a motorbike,' she decided. 'I'll ride it right across America and get a job as a Californian beach guard.'

Time crept by. Occasionally a family of holiday-makers would come in, take a look and back out again. Each time Jo and Jaz thought they'd rather go with them.

After about half an hour the bikers started to leave

and other customers began to drift in. 'They look more like students,' Jaz whispered.

Jo could not be sure, but she thought one or two had been to Abby's party. They certainly knew each other and they knew Mick. They shouted and joked to each other across the tables and the café began to take on a different feel. These were clearly the regulars.

'Did you hear about Dimitri?' asked a guy behind Jo to the café in general.

'No.' 'What about him?' 'Is he still around?' asked several voices.

'Not any more,' answered the first.

Dimitri? Where had she heard that name, Jo wondered. Dim—the guy on the fire escape. The one who quoted Tennyson and gazed at the moon.

'He's a goner,' continued the voice. 'Got high the other night and went for a walk on the cliffs. Wandered too near the edge, they said. I reckon he was trying to fly.'

'Poor old Dim,' said someone.

'He was crazy,' said another. The first voice was describing how he had been found at the bottom. Jo tried to blot out the gruesome details. Dim, who still believed he could find a newer world. Dimitri, who had been found in a mangled heap on the undercliff path. He would never find what he was looking for now.

Jo unblocked her ears and opened her eyes. She hadn't realized she had closed them. It was a shock to find Jaz was missing, no longer sitting opposite. She turned to see her at the counter. Mick was serving, looking, thought Jo, a bit shaken.

Jaz returned with a coke and a triumphant smile.

'You could have got me one,' said Jo and Jaz recoiled at her angry tone.

'Sorry. Here have it. I didn't have enough money for two.' She leant forward and whispered. 'See that couple over there? Mick's just passed them something. It looked like little white packets. That's drugs, right?'

'Right.'

'I was watching, that's why I went to the counter. And he said . . . Listen,' she pulled Jo closer. 'He said he'd run out now and he'd be getting some more tomorrow. He said he'd be back here with fresh supplies by lunch-time.' She sat back with pride. Suddenly she looked at Jo. 'What's the matter with you? You look like you've seen a ghost.'

It was the ghost of a poet on a fire escape. Jo sat silent on the bus going back, haunted not only by Dimitri but also by fear. Fear that something, that terrible unnamed something, would carry Abby off in the same way. But they were hauntings she couldn't bring herself to explain, and she forced herself to listen while Jaz explained her plan.

'Look, I've got to go to church tomorrow. I know you think it's silly, but I promised I'd be in the choir. So listen, if you come over to Brighton and wait around till he leaves and then follow him, I'll slip out of church as soon as it finishes and watch out by the footbridge, just in case. That way, if you miss him, I might see him, or vice versa.'

Jo felt sure it couldn't be as simple as it sounded, but her numbed brain couldn't figure out why. She didn't need to worry. Jaz was working through every eventuality.

'Oh, he doesn't drive, does he?'

'Don't think so.'

'Or ride a bike?'

'How should I know?'

'I suppose he'll leave from home. Where does he live?'

'Dunno.'

'Bother. Well, we could try looking him up in the phone book.'

Surprisingly, Jaz's plan worked. The phone book showed two Valentinos. The first gave no answer, but the second did.

'Is Mick in?' asked Jo. ('It's all right,' she explained to Jaz, 'because we know he isn't.') 'Could you tell me where he lives now then? ... Oh, just a friend ... Right, 14 Whitewalls Court,' she repeated, scrabbling for pencil and paper. 'Thanks a lot. Bye ... There, 14 Whitewalls Court, Windmill Road.'

'Great,' said Jaz. 'Make sure you're there nice and early tomorrow.'

10

On the Trail

Jo was there early, far too early. She hid her bike under some dirty bushes and then lurked for what seemed like an eternity behind them.

I never used to do all this hanging around until I met Jasmine Walcott, she thought.

It began to drizzle. She dived into a phone-box on the corner of the road. Luckily hardly anyone seemed to make phone calls on Sunday mornings in Windmill Road. One woman paced up and down outside, glared at Jo and left in disgust. An old man, more persistent, banged on the glass and Jo had to make a great pantomime of finishing an imaginary call and leaving the box. It was a relief. Three-quarters of an hour in a phone-box is a very long time.

Right, that's it. I'm giving up, she decided, and made to go. But somehow she didn't.

This is ridiculous, she told herself, taking up her place in the phone-box again.

Yes, but what about Abby? her other self argued back.

Well, what about her? the tired, hungry self replied. If we stopped Mick, she could get drugs somewhere else.

But it might save someone else from starting.

The arguments raged in her head, so much so that she almost didn't notice when Mick came out of Whitewalls Court. But something made her glance up just at the right moment, and duck her head away as he passed by. She let him get a few yards away, then swung out of the phone-box and grabbed her bike. If he did what she was expecting, he would go down to the crossroads and catch the Shoreham bus.

He did.

She waited until he had safely boarded the bus, and then followed furiously. She didn't want to lose him now. It was a strange bike journey, pedalling crazily to keep pace with the bus, with sudden halts in between. But somehow she managed and, true to plan, he got off at the footbridge. He fooled her by turning abruptly right instead of left, but it was only to get some cigarettes at a newsagent's. Then he set off across the bridge.

This was a problem. How far to hang back? The bridge was long and straight with no corners to hide behind. She gave him a good start and just hoped he wouldn't turn round. He didn't. He carried, she noted, an empty haversack—for supplies, no doubt. At the end of the bridge he turned right along the river path that led to *Trade Winds*.

But what had happened to Jaz? There had been no sign of her in the town, but now as Jo turned off the bridge, Jaz swung into step beside her. It was a good moment—two friends together, no need for words.

Mick was slowing now, looking from left to right.

'Ditch the bike,' hissed Jaz and obediently Jo laid it on the grass.

Just in time, too. Because the next minute Mick was stopping and turning to look back. Jaz and Jo threw themselves down the bank and into some bushes. They crouched in the prickly undergrowth for about a minute before Jo cautiously raised her head.

Mick had disappeared.

They dashed along the path to the spot where Mick had last been seen. It was right next to Number 23—the 'smuggler's' house. Had they been right all along? But the house and all the surrounding houses and boats were locked and silent.

Now what?

'Lost something, girls?' asked a voice behind them. They turned to see Sebastian, apparently ready for a jog, his golden hair tousled, and his tanned muscles looking their impressive best.

Jaz waited for Jo to speak. Jo waited for Jaz to speak. Both were momentarily dumbstruck—by Sebastian's warm, smiling presence, by the problem of explaining what, or who, they had lost, and by a sudden dark suspicion which flitted through each of their minds.

Jo found her voice first. 'Well, yeah. You haven't seen a sort of skinny bloke, have you? Longish dark hair, needs a shave, with a haversack on his back.'

Sebastian considered. 'No, I haven't, but then I did only just step outside. Bit jet-lagged, I'm afraid. What's the trouble, this guy been bothering you?'

'No, it's not that . . .' Jo paused. 'We think he's selling drugs.'

Sebastian looked at them both, raising his eyebrows. 'Whatever makes you think that?' he asked, his hands on his hips.

99

Jo started to explain as best she could. She told Sebastian how they'd seen the packets change hands in the café. She didn't mention Abby.

'We think he might be getting them from that house over there,' Jaz added, pointing to Number 23.

'D'you know,' Sebastian looked concerned and thoughtful, 'now you mention it, I think I have seen a guy like that going in there. And that place has some pretty strange goings-on. But don't get mixed up in things, girls. If you're worried, you ought to tell the police.'

'But . . .' began Jo, and tailed off uncertainly.

'Oh, listen, if you're worried they won't believe you . . . Is that it? Well, how about if I phone the police for you, just tell them about our suspicions. No, it's no problem. I'll do it now.'

He turned back on to his houseboat and Jaz and Jo began to follow.

'No, you'd better hang on out here. Bachelor living, I'm afraid. Bit of a mess.'

He pushed the door to, but they could hear him calling, 'Stay in bed, darling, I've just got to make a call.'

'That's it. He's got a woman in there,' Jo sniggered. Jaz felt herself flush with embarrassment.

In a few minutes he was out again. 'They were very grateful for the tip-off and they'll be mounting a watch. Now, if you'll excuse me,' he came out and shut the door behind him, 'I've got to fight off this jet lag.'

They watched him jog away down the path, a picture of glowing fitness. Jo suddenly realized that she felt damp, tired and hungry. 'Well, that's it then. Might as well go home.'

Jaz hesitated. 'You don't think we ought to wait, just to check that Mick does come out of the house?'

Oh no, not more waiting, thought Jo. She shivered.

'It'll probably only be a few minutes, then we'll know for sure,' insisted Jaz.

Jo had to hand it to Jaz. When she decided to do something she was certainly determined. 'OK, just a few more minutes,' she said reluctantly.

But the minutes lengthened and the drizzle thickened into heavy rain.

'Oh, come on,' said Jo at last. 'This is daft.'

'We can't give up now,' said Jaz fiercely. But Jo was already marching along the path to *Trade Winds*.

Jaz watched her go. 'I was only doing this for you,' she silently told Jo's back. 'And I bunked out of church before the end. I don't think God minds 'cos I did the choir bit I promised, but there'll still be trouble when I get back.' The thought made her cross, and the rain ran down the back of her neck.

The crossness and wetness made her bold. On a sudden whim she crept down into the garden and crouched below the windows of Number 23. Even if there was nothing to see, perhaps she could hear some evidence.

What she heard was a banging noise—thump, thump thump—and a strange low moaning.

A mixture of cold fear and curiosity gripped her. The fear told her to get out, but the curiosity made her raise her head silently and carefully to the corner of the window.

It was the strange boy who was moaning. He was crouching on a chair, rocking back and forth, each time knocking his head against the wall. Again and again he banged his head. He clasped and unclasped his hands, and every so often looked up to a corner of the room and moaned.

Jaz followed his eyes, and what she saw made her gasp. The man—his father—lay sprawled on the floor. Was he dead? Had the boy killed him? Had Mick killed him? Was Mick still hiding inside, or had he ever been there at all? Tell the police, she thought. Get an ambulance. But was that a movement? Suppose he's alive now, but dies while I've gone?

She tried the door. It was locked. She tried the windows. All locked. She picked her way over rubbish sacks and rusting engine parts to the back of the house. She rattled the back door. That too was locked. Jaz tried every window and stumbled her way round again to the front. There was no sign of Mick.

What was the boy's name? Gary, that was it. She remembered the look of pride on the man's face. 'Gary . . . my son,' he had said.

'Gary, Gary, come here.' Gary continued rocking but lifted his head. There was no hint of recognition.

'Come here, Gary.' Jaz tapped on the window and then on the door. He got up and shambled over.

'Open the door, Gary,' commanded Jaz in a trembling voice. She tapped the outside of the lock.

'Here, turn it.' She heard a lot of fumbling. 'Here Gary, open the door.' More fumbling, and then, amazingly, the sound of a key turning. 'Brilliant, Gary, well done.'

But the door still wouldn't open. Something held it firmly at the top. There must be a bolt. Jaz tapped the top of the door. 'Here, Gary, here. Slide the bolt.' There was silence. Then a moaning and thumping as if Gary had resumed the head banging against the door. 'Just push the bolt, Gary. Up here.'

The thumping stopped. A scrabbling behind the door. The sound of a rusty bolt being scraped back. Jaz pushed and the door opened. The boy stood, helpless and harmless, and she pushed past him into the room. Oh, God, please don't let it be a dead body.

It wasn't. The man was breathing—laboriously, as if each gasp was a struggle. There was no blood. Thank you, God. But now what? The man opened his eyes, stared at her wildly and tried to speak. Whatever it was, she couldn't understand. With a groan, he lapsed back into unconsciousness. Now what? Sit him up, turn him over? No, don't move him, he might have broken bones. What good were all those first aid classes? He still might die. Now, while she was kneeling here dithering. Then on a cabinet she spotted the phone. Her shaking fingers stabbed out 999.

'Fire, police or ambulance?' said a voice.

'Ambulance, please,' said Jaz.

Jo heard the howl of the ambulance as she came out of *Trade Winds*. Drier now and guiltier, she was coming to see what had happened to Jaz—and to retrieve her abandoned bike.

She watched the progress of the flashing blue light over the road bridge, and heard the wailing change direction and get louder as it came toward the Beach. She caught a glimpse as it flashed past on Beach Road. The siren trailed away and stopped.

No sign of Jaz. She must have gone. Jo picked up her bike and cycled home, deflated. No more excitement. Nothing to do. She didn't hear the paramedics rushing up the path behind her, and she didn't see as they turned in to a very familiar house.

'Could be a heart attack,' the ambulance man had said. 'Can't be certain.'

'What about the lad?' the ambulance woman had said. 'Is he a friend of yours?'

'Not exactly,' said Jaz, stroking Gary's twisting hands. She had found it calmed him a bit and stopped the awful head banging.

'We'd better get Social Services out. Can you cope with him for a little while?'

'That's all right,' said Jaz. She knew what to do with people who were lost and lonely on Sunday lunch-times. 'I'll take him home to Mum and Dad.'

11

Shiny Happy Person

'Dad phoned,' said Mum, as Jo clattered down into the cabin.

Dad! It was Sunday! She was supposed to be meeting him today. She'd completely forgotten.

'He can't make it this week. He promised next week. But I shouldn't hold your breath. We all know your father's promises, don't we?'

'Yeah,' said Jo dully, sinking wearily on to the cabin bench.

'He wanted to speak to you, but you weren't here. Where on earth have you been all morning? And what's this pile of wet clothes?'

'Just out. It rained.' Jo turned the telly on.

'He says Abby's staying in London with him for the holidays.'

'Huh?'

'Turn that thing down. Your sister's gone to London. Staying with your dad.'

'Did he say I could come?'

'No.'

'Oh.' Jo flicked channels blankly. Politicians argued, a vicar was being sincere, brave RAF chaps were going off to fight the Hun, in 'The Little House on the Prairie' the family were sitting down together round a pink check tablecloth. Yuck—whatever happened to the real world?

'Look,' Mum came in from the galley, wiping her hands, 'it's not that he doesn't want you. But he's got the office in the day and his precious jazz band in the evenings. He's only having Abby because she can look after herself.'

'I can look after myself.'

'Jo, you're only just fourteen. I'm sorry. We just can't afford a proper holiday but we'll take some days out. I'll take you up to town if you like. We'll go shopping, we might get some last-minute tickets for a show.'

'Thanks.'

Only fourteen! What did Mum know? I can look after myself better than Abby, thought Jo. And who are you kidding? She's always been Dad's favourite and you know it.

She flipped channels again. In the Little House the family were sitting down to homemade apple pie.

'D'you wanna go down the chippy?' asked Mum.

'Can we feed another one for lunch, Mum?' asked Jaz.

Somehow she had dragged this strange, shambling boy home. It had been all right over the footbridge, but she had needed all her strength to hang on to him when they came to the busy main road. He seemed to have no idea of traffic. Once he broke free and wandered into the middle of the road. A car had swerved and hooted and screeched to a halt, and an angry woman had shouted at Jaz as she'd tried to rescue him.

It wasn't that he minded coming. He had moaned and rocked as his father was taken out, but once the ambulance had driven off, he seemed to forget. He was quite docile as Jaz led him out of the door, and trotted along beside her obediently. It was just that now and then something inexplicable would grab his attention and he would dash to see it. He reminded Jaz of a toddler like Clifford, except that this toddler was bigger and stronger than she was. When Clifford had a tantrum it was funny, when Gary had one it was dangerous.

'Who is it, love?' asked Mum, stirring the gravy. 'Where did you get to after church?'

Jaz drew a deep breath. 'Well, it's a bit hard to explain . . .' Gary rushed past her into the kitchen. Mum turned, startled, and Gary knocked the gravy packet out of her hand. Granules scattered across the floor.

The object of his interest was the mobile hanging from the kitchen ceiling—sun, moon and stars of shiny paper. Alex had made it years ago in Sunday School and it had hung in the kitchen ever since. Gary grabbed it and pulled it down from the ceiling. A shower of plaster came away with the drawing pin. He stood motionless, holding the mobile in front of him and staring fascinated as shining constellations twirled before his eyes.

'You were saying,' said Mum, 'that it was a bit hard to explain . . .'

The explanation was truthful, Jaz told herself, as far as it went. She had slipped out to see Jo who was upset because her sister wasn't well. She'd noticed Gary very distressed and gone in and found his dad lying on the floor.

'I gave the ambulance man our number. They said Social Services would phone as soon as they'd got somewhere for him to go. He's called Gary.'

Mum furrowed her brows at this garbled account, but the doorbell came to Jaz's rescue. Mum handed her the dustpan and brush and went to welcome the Trevinnicks to lunch.

It was not an easy mealtime. Gary ate with his fingers and slopped food around. Every so often he would moan and rock and push the plate aside. He would get up and wander round—searching, it seemed, for his missing father and his familiar surroundings.

Jaz sat there in an agony of embarrassment and just wished she'd remembered who it was who was coming to lunch today. The Trevinnicks lived in a posh new bungalow at the back of town. They'd been at the chapel for twenty years and didn't approve of 'all this loud emotionalism'.

Dad believed that sharing your food with people broke down all sorts of barriers, but today Jaz could see them rising before her very eyes.

It was a relief when the bell rang and Jo was on the doorstep.

'Sorry. I shouldn't have gone off like... Who on earth...? Whatever's he doing here?'

'Mum, Jo's here. We're taking Gary out for a walk,' said Jaz quickly, and hauled Gary out of the door before anyone had a chance to argue.

'You're not going to believe this. But what happened was...'

Gary shambled between them, still clutching the

The Bellview mob were in residence at the café. 'Sad boy, sad boy,' they chanted as Gary rifled through a rubbish bin. 'Which one of you two fancies him then?'

'I fancy him more than I fancy you,' said Jo, 'but that's not saying much.'

'Help me,' hissed Jaz, hopelessly trying to pull him away.

'Nah, let him,' said Jo. 'He's happy.'

She got three ice-creams with her chip money, and Gary, delighted to have found five more shinies, made an immense mess with his. It ended when he dropped it upside down on the pavement and made an enormous fuss when he wasn't allowed to pick it up.

'Oh, have mine,' said Jaz desperately. 'I'm going to the loo.'

She didn't really need to go. It was just an escape, from the staring faces, from the embarrassing, inexplicable behaviour that never let up.

Poor man, she thought, as she sat in the cold smelly cubicle. No wonder he was bad-tempered if he had to cope with that all the time.

Poor man? He could be a drugs dealer! But that wasn't his son's fault, and it didn't change the fact that he was dangerously ill. What had happened to him, she wondered. He could be dead. Or was he alive, and worrying what on earth had happened to his son?

'Come on,' she said urgently to a surprised Jo. 'I think we'd better be getting back.'

'I've had a phone call from Social Services,' said Pastor Walcott. 'The boy's father's in the County General. Heart attack. In Intensive Care, but he's through the worst. He was conscious again and

111

desperate to know about his son. So the nurse put me through and we had a bit of a chat. The name's Ted Carter. Sad sort of character. Doesn't seem to be any other family, just him and the lad. I promised we'd take Gary to visit tomorrow. And a social worker just phoned. She said they hadn't found a place for the boy yet. I told her not to worry, we could manage. She was a bit sniffy about just who we were, but when she found out Mum was a registered child-minder and I was a man of the cloth, she decided to bend the rules. I said we had a spare bedroom.'

'We haven't,' said Jaz.

'Well, since he's your guest, we were sure you wouldn't mind giving up your bedroom.'

Good old Dad, thought Jaz, as she bedded down on the sofa.

What an amazing man, thought Jo as she tumbled wearily into the bunk of her creaking cabin. Taking on other people's troubles as if they were his own. My dad can't even be bothered with his own family. The thought threw a sudden punch at her stomach.

What the heck. It had been a long day. The boat rocked gently and the water lapped comfortingly the other side of the creaking timbers. She drifted into sleep and dreamt of picking up interminable 'shinies' from the sand, while in a phone-box in the middle of the beach, Mick sold drugs to an endless stream of bikers in black leather.

12

Blood Brothers

The following afternoon an overloaded and creaking old Vauxhall set off for Brighton with Pastor Walcott at the wheel. Mrs Walcott and Alex were having a lift to the shops, but in the back Jaz and Jo were wedged either side of Gary to make sure he behaved.

Jo hadn't wanted to go—'I hate hospitals. It's the smell.' But Jaz had persuaded her—'You've gotta come. You're so much better with Gary than anyone else.'

In fact, Jo had been at the Walcotts' looking after Gary ever since Jaz had phoned her early that morning. 'He's really upset. He doesn't know where he is. I think he's looking for his dad. All he does is keep rocking backwards and forwards.'

Well, there was nothing else to do in the school holidays, thought Jo. She had tried Number 23 on the way, thinking to find Gary some clothes or perhaps a toy. But the door must have been locked behind the ambulance men. She thought about climbing in, but there were, she noticed, even more plain-clothes men with binoculars on the far bank this morning. She glanced at the *Shangri-La* as she passed. It looked deserted and Sebastian's Range Rover had gone from the car park at the end of the green.

At the Walcotts' Jo had found some tin foil and glue, and coaxed Gary into sticking glittering paper shapes all over cardboard boxes. He especially liked the empty gravy-mix canister and spent a long time covering it with scrunched up foil.

'Look, this is a super deluxe model shiny,' proclaimed Jo.

So the day had passed relatively calmly, and now they were at the hospital and about to enter the Intensive Care ward. Jo had expected an atmosphere of steel and white porcelain, and horrible apparatus that dripped and blipped, but they found Ted Carter propped up in bed in a cheerful side ward with yellow walls and flowery curtains.

He smiled as Gary charged in, with Jo trying vainly to hold him back. The smile drained away as he saw Pastor Walcott and Jaz behind them.

'Are you the people who've been looking after my son?'

'Yes. Good to meet you. I'm Daniel Walcott,' he held out his hand, 'and this is Jasmine, my daughter.'

The man in the bed ignored the proffered handshake and turned toward his son. Gary, however, having found his father, had decided the cartoons on the TV in the corner were far more interesting.

'He's been very good, and we're managing fine. Jodi here's been an excellent helper. Social Services say they should find somewhere in a day or two, but in the meantime it's no problem and . . .' Pastor Walcott broke off, even his jovial warmth chilled by the hostility that met his eyes.

'It may not be a problem 'for you,' muttered Mr Carter. He closed his eyes and sunk his head back into the pillow.

'I'm sorry. I wasn't meaning to . . . It must have been a terrible time for you. I just meant that Mrs Walcott and I are glad to be of help. You needn't feel bad about it. You could say it's part of my job, if you like.'

'I don't like,' mumbled Mr Carter, his eyes remaining shut.

Jaz and Jo exchanged puzzled glances.

It's because they're black, that's all there is to it, thought Jo. Or is it because of his guilty secret? He's got the drugs and he thinks we've discovered them.

Jaz knew what it was. The colour of her skin. She was often conscious of it, mostly through things people said. They weren't necessarily nasty, mostly just thoughtless, but you knew they had slotted you in a category marked different, one step down from them.

But this man . . . He looked at them with a sort of revulsion, as if they were dirty or carrying some awful disease. She glanced at Dad uncertainly and he felt for her hand and squeezed it.

There was a silence, broken only by the raucous squawkings of the cartoon characters.

Mr Carter opened his eyes and struggled to sit up. 'I appreciate your help,' he said coldly, 'but it won't be necessary. They say I'm making excellent progress and I'm feeling much better already. You can leave Gary here with me and I'll take him home later.'

As if to prove his point he swung his legs over the side of the bed, but his bravado drained away with the colour from his face, and he swayed uneasily as he tried to rise.

Then Pastor Walcott did what Jo thought was a very brave thing. Gently but firmly he helped the angry man back into bed.

'I'm sorry, Mr Carter. I realize we're not quite the people you'd like to look after your son. I'm sure they'll find you someone else as soon as they can, and if it helps I'll try and make sure they do. But for the moment, you really don't have the choice. You're a sick man.'

Mr Carter stared at the Pastor's hand on his shoulder. He shrugged irritably. Pastor Walcott left it there a moment longer before removing it.

'You seem a very angry man, Mr Carter, I don't know why. But I do know all this anger isn't doing you any good at all. Not in your condition.'

'What do you know about my condition?'

'I know, believe me. I've had my share of heart problems. That awful pressure on the chest, breathlessness, having to stop halfway up the stairs. I've been there. Funny, isn't it? My blood flows just the same as yours does underneath.'

Jo felt her indignation boiling over. 'Look 'ere. They're really nice people, honestly. You ought to be grateful. They're dead kind and patient even with your Gary. And he can be a right pain sometimes, believe me!'

The man almost smiled.

As if on cue, the cartoons finished and Gary got up. He roamed the room, trying the radio knobs on the wall, the window catches, the curtains. Then he saw a bright metal object tucked away on a shelf. He made a dive for it and bore it back triumphantly to his father.

'That's a funny-shaped bottle,' said Jaz, trying to be polite.

'It's what they pee into,' hissed Jo.

'Shiny,' said Gary.

Even Mr Carter managed a laugh.

After that things got better. Jo told him about the 'shinies' in the park, and Jaz retold her story, perfected at every telling, of how she'd seen Gary distressed at the window and come to his aid.

'You're a thoughtful young woman,' said Mr Carter, and Jaz flushed guiltily at the deception. Even now the police might be on their way to arrest him.

'... Even so, I'm afraid I don't like taking help and Gary's best with me. I'll be out in a couple of days and in the meantime ... Thank you.'

To Jo's ears the last words were almost spat out, but Pastor Walcott caught the effort beneath them.

'It's OK. Look after yourself, now, and you'll be back to normal in no time. Shall we bring him in to visit tomorrow?'

Mr Carter nodded, as if the supreme effort of that thank you had driven all other words from him.

'Time to go, Gary,' said Jo.

Here comes the difficult bit, thought Jaz. Dear God, please let him be all right now.

Gary wasn't all right. He began to struggle as he realized they were taking him, whether from his father or the TV they couldn't tell. But miraculously a nurse was there the second they got up. She drew the curtains round the bed.

'Blood tests, Mr Carter, now be a good boy for me ...'

'Hold tight and stay calm,' said Jo and together they dragged the kicking, hitting bundle of fury from the ward, without his father seeing a thing.

Outside the hospital Gary stopped abruptly. He had noticed another rubbish bin.

Thank you, God, thought Jaz.

'Thank God that's over,' said Jo.

A couple of days later a social worker in a neat little Citroën came to take Gary away to a 'proper' foster home.

Jo, who had almost taken up residence at the Walcotts' as volunteer helper, felt quite sad to see him go.

'Here you are.' She gave the social worker a large carrier bag. 'He'll need these.'

The bag was full of old tin cans, with a few cereal boxes pasted with tin foil shoved in for good measure.

The young woman was terribly polite. '... But really, we can't take rubbish like this,' she said.

'But it's important to him,' protested Jo.

'I'm sorry,' said the weary young woman, 'but I've already been to his home and collected some clothes and suitable games.'

'Was there ...?' began Jaz, and stopped.

'You didn't find anything ... unusual, did you?' asked Jo casually.

'No,' the woman looked faintly puzzled. 'Bit of a mess, but then you'd expect that from a man. All the same, Mr Carter seems a devoted enough father.' She turned to her sheaf of papers. 'Now, you're not relatives?' She looked up. 'No, no, of course not. Can I put friends?'

'Yes,' said Pastor Walcott. 'I hope so.'

Gary was happily watching cartoon videos with

Alex and Clifford and appeared to be on best behaviour. But the woman's brisk, 'Now Gareth, I'm going to take you somewhere very special,' met with no response at all.

'Would you mind for just a minute, boys?' She turned the TV off. It was not a good move. Gary turned it on again, she turned it off, and so Gary aimed a large and deliberate kick at her backside. Jo stood back from the full-scale battle that followed. 'Let her struggle,' she thought, but as Gary got more and more upset and confused she could no longer watch. She slipped out of the room, dragging Jaz with her.

They returned seconds later with a gold-wrapped object. 'Oi Gary,' said Jo. 'Wanna choc ice?'

Gary lunged towards her. 'OK, sunshine. But you've gotta have it where I say.'

She backed out towards the smart Citroën with Gary behind her and the dishevelled social worker in pursuit.

'Keys,' demanded Jo.

The social worker unlocked the car and Jo slid in. 'Come on Gary, it's in here,' called Jo. Gary followed her into the back seat. 'Brill, Gary. Here you are, then.' She unwrapped the choc ice. 'Sorry mate, I hate to do this to you.' Jo slid out of the car the other side. 'Bye Gary, bye for now.'

For a second he glanced up. 'Bye Jo,' he said.

It was the nicest thing that had happened to her for days. Somewhere in Gary's jumbled, malfunctioning brain he had registered her as someone special—he knew her name.

She felt almost empty as the car drove away. Then she laughed, 'I bet he gets ice-cream all over the seats.'

What Jaz felt was more like relief. But even so, she was sad. At least it had been a diversion. The long summer holidays stretched ahead with no money and nothing to do.

Except, she remembered—there was still the mystery of the smuggler.

13

River Rats

'Sebastian's back,' said Jo, as they walked along the river path a week or so later. 'I saw his flashy car. Let's go and ask if he's heard anything.'

Sebastian's Range Rover was indeed back, but Sebastian was missing. The men with binoculars had disappeared too.

Jaz and Jo wandered aimlessly for a while, until Jo had an idea. 'What about his fishing boat?'

They made their way over the footbridge and into the town. Down the thundering main road, past the fish market, the car auction and the bin lorry depot, they found the dusty wall. The door was open. They pushed into the dingy scrapyard and found *Peggy Sue* moored alongside. Sebastian was on deck, fiddling with some ropes and talking into the mobile phone wedged on his shoulder.

'Tonight it is, then.' He looked up sharply at the crunch of feet on gravel. 'Gotta go. Great to hear from you. So glad you phoned. Bye.'

He smiled, 'Hi girls, come to give me a hand?'

'Hi,' said Jo. 'We just wondered if you'd heard anything?'

He looked blank.

'From the police.'

The smile flickered. 'Should I have?'

'After you phoned,' reminded Jaz.

'Of course.' The smile returned. 'But no, I'm afraid I've been away for the last few days. Incredibly busy. But the miserable guy in the house seems to have scarpered—milk bottles outside and that.'

'Yes, we know,' explained Jo, and chronicled the events of the last few days. She ended with a description of the men with binoculars, and how they'd all gone away.

'So we know they've been watching and we just wondered if they'd found anything.'

'I'd be quite interested to know that myself,' said Sebastian, busying himself with the ropes again.

'Oh well, sorry to bother you,' said Jo as they made to leave. At the door, she turned. 'Did you really mean it about wanting a hand?'

Sebastian paused for a moment. He seemed pre-occupied. Then he brightened, 'OK. Why not?'

He threw the rope at Jo. 'Grab an end, I could do with some help unravelling these.'

After the ropes were neatly coiled he gave them both paintbrushes and a shared pot of grey paint.

'I know it looks dreary, but she badly needs weather-proofing. This is just undercoat. I'll put the bright colours on later.'

They painted over the bright orange cabin, and around the boat's blue rim. Jaz paused when she came to the boat's name, and a set of numbers.

'Don't worry. Go right over it for now,' said Sebastian. 'I can paint it back in later.'

'Have you been fishing yet?' asked Jo as she slopped paint with abandon.

'Not yet. Too busy. Had some big shows to arrange. Have to confirm all the bookings now for Christmas. But I've got my first charter trip arranged—mackerel fishing—tonight, in fact. That's why I'm down here now.'

'You don't book dancers, do you?' asked Jaz timidly. Her painting was slower and more careful, but then she did have her newest white T-shirt on.

'Dancers? Yeah, now and again. Got a couple of great troupes I use. Hot Ice, heard of them?'

'No, but you see,' Jaz hesitated. 'That's what I really want to be—a dancer. I just wondered if you knew anyone, you know, locally, or even in London, who'd take me on.'

Sebastian looked amused. 'Ambitious, eh? You're a bit young. Preacher's kid, aren't you?'

'Yes, but . . .' Jaz looked defensive.

'She's brilliant at gymnastics,' put in Jo. 'She gets medals and stuff.'

'Yes, but dancing's different. It's a dirty old world, showbiz. Not the place for religious types. I don't think your mummy and daddy would approve.'

'God made dancing,' said Jaz stoutly. 'He approves. I can dance to the glory of God.'

Sebastian smiled. 'I don't think that's quite how my friends see it. But it's as good a view as any other. Come on then, give us a demo!'

He reached down to a battered radio in the cabin and jabbed the button. A disco beat disturbed the quiet riverside and seagulls flapped upwards.

'Come on, then, young Jasmine. Give us a twirl.'

For a moment Jaz stood frozen with self-consciousness. Then, with a supreme act of determination, she began to move, stepping carefully with the beat. Jo clapped her on. Gradually Jaz gained confidence, her movements swelling until she forgot herself and the boat could not contain her. She leapt to the quay as the tempo quickened. Faster and fiercer she whirled. Clouds of dust rose around her—the sun caught in them and danced with her. Above in a deep blue heaven, the seagulls wheeled and dipped.

The music stopped abruptly and Jaz ended with a triumphant back-flip. She stood panting and exhilarated. Jo applauded wildly, but Sebastian stood motionless, paintbrush in hand.

'Well?' Jo prompted. 'She's good, isn't she?'

Sebastian didn't answer for a moment. Then he stirred. 'Sorry,' he said absently. 'It reminded me of ... something. Have you ever caught a memory of a place you've never been?'

Jo looked blank. 'Dunno ... But she was good, wasn't she?'

Sebastian switched off his thoughts and offered a gentlemanly hand to help Jaz back on board. 'I don't think I'd recognize the glory of God if it came and hit me in the face.' He smiled at her. 'But you're what I'd call a lovely little mover. I can recognize that.'

'I got a lot wrong,' said Jaz.

'Oh, technical stuff,' Sebastian waved his arm. 'You can learn that. You've got something you can't learn—spirit, simplicity. There's the makings of a good dancer there.'

Jaz's shy face lit up.

'And, as I'm sure you know, you've got the makings of quite a beauty.'

No one, ever, had called her that before. She didn't quite believe it. Sebastian—glamorous, jet-setting, handsome Sebastian—had called her beautiful. She stored it away, a golden thought, as a comfort against hard times.

'Look, I'm not sure there's anything I can do,' went on Sebastian. 'It's not really my line of country, but give me your address and phone number, anyway.'

Jaz found an eye-pencil and the back of a bus ticket and scribbled it eagerly.

'Great, no guarantees—but I'll keep you in mind, I promise.'

The radio struck up a new tune, a bouncy, silly sort of number, and Sebastian started a hand jive. And then they were all at it, clapping and waving, stomping and jigging until they collapsed in gales of laughter and covered with grey paint smudges.

But then the magic broke, as it always seemed to with Sebastian, when the phone started bleeping. In the first few words of muttered conversation, his whole body changed from relaxed and sprawled over the deck to tense and huddled over the phone. He turned back to the girls, but only to shoo them away with an irritable gesture.

'I think that's our cue to leave,' said Jo, wiping her paint-stained hands on an oily rag.

'Three, OK, three,' Sebastian was saying as they crept away.

The sun was going down as they wandered into the town.

'Let's go to your place and doss,' said Jo.

'Why don't we go to your place?' objected Jaz. 'I haven't been there for ages.'

It was funny—to Jo her home seemed silent and dull, compared to the comings and goings and noisy banter of Jaz's. She forgot that to a land-dweller the 'river rats', as they called themselves, were a strange and exotic breed.

Mum was out when they got to *Trade Winds* so they fixed themselves Jo's favourite, 'a humungous fry-up', and sat on deck munching appreciatively, ketchup drips mingling with the grey paint on their hands and T-shirts.

This was when the river was at its nicest. If you looked downstream, everything was bathed in a gentle golden glow. If you looked up-river the rocking dinghies and distant traffic on the bridge were silhouetted against the sparkling water and the dying sun.

The other boat owners were enjoying it too. Next door Cath and Joe, who came as hippies in the Sixties and never left, were tending their garden. It was a strange garden, planted in a higgledy group of loos, bidets and urinals on their tiny patch of bank. Marigolds, sweet peas and daisies grew in profusion, and Cath and Joe were always raiding skips to add another free plant pot to their collection.

On the other side, Charlie Finn, the writer, was entertaining a group of friends. Several rounds of beer had already been consumed and the conversation was getting louder.

'You are lucky,' said Jaz, 'living here.'

Yes, thought Jo, it did have its good points. There was a sort of comradeship among the boat people. They'd always help you out in a fix. And there were some real characters down here: like Mad Arthur who thought his boat was still part of World War Two and was occasionally seen to wear a tin hat, or Nessie and Gwen, the sisters whose boat was an unofficial cat sanctuary.

The neighbouring land-dwellers in their neat riverside flats and bungalows looked down on the boat people. They weren't tidy, they said, and sometimes they were noisy.

But on evenings like this, with children playing on the green, barbecue smoke rising from back gardens and on almost every boat deck a cat curled up in a patch of warm sun, mud-dwellers and land-dwellers were united in their pleasure.

The thing that drew them here, the river, continued its lazy, never-ending flow. Out on the mud-flats, another community lived out its life. Seagulls, coots, moorhens, bobbing on the water or drifting above, descending now and then to squabble over territory or scraps of food.

Jo gazed idly along the mud-flats. A flashing glint of light caught her eye. It came from under the footbridge, somewhere among the reeds and stubby bushes. She stared as the glint came and went again. It was, she made out, binoculars, catching and reflecting the dying sun. They seemed to be trained towards the houses and the bank.

'Hey look,' she pointed Jaz in the right direction. 'There is still someone watching. How about we go and see what they've discovered?'

The man with binoculars was startled and somewhat cross when two girls slid down the bank behind him.

'Sssh,' he hissed. 'Get down.'

He didn't lower his binoculars and the girls strained to see where they were pointing.

'Have you discovered anything?' whispered Jo after a pause.

''Fraid not,' he whispered back. 'They seem to have flown.'

'Are you the only one here now?'

'Seems like it. I was too late really. The others reported some really good sightings.'

'So, will you keep watching?'

'I'll stay for a while. But it was a pretty rare chance and I think they've gone for the summer now.'

'But who was it?' asked Jo. 'Did you get any evidence?'

The man looked faintly puzzled. 'Evidence? No, I'm not a photos man myself. I just enjoy watching.'

It was Jaz's turn to be puzzled. 'But who was it?'

'Caspian tern. Wonderful creature—blown off course by the gales—chance of a lifetime. Too late, I reckon, but never mind.'

'You're not a policeman, then?'

'Policeman? No, I'm a butcher. Why'd you ask?'

'Oh . . . we just wondered. The other people with binoculars—were they policemen?'

'Well, that I couldn't tell you. We only meet each other at times like this. Funny thing, you see the same faces pop up all over the country—St Ives, Berwick—real twitchers'll go anywhere and word travels fast when there's a good sighting. But as to what they do the rest of the time, I don't know. We only talk about the birds.'

'Oh.' Jaz and Jo looked at each other, not sure whether to giggle or groan.

'Hey look, I think it's . . . Yes, marsh warbler. Now that's worth coming for. And there's his mate.' The butcher in the green anorak was getting excited. 'Wonderful, what a beauty. Here, want a look?'

He handed Jo the binoculars. 'There, by that clump of reeds, just back from those timbers, the sunken boat. Isn't he a beauty?'

It looked like a fairly ordinary brown bird to Jo, but it would have been rude to say so.

'Lovely, great, thanks. We'd better be going now. Good luck with the, er, twitching.'

They scrambled up the bank and ran all the way back to *Trade Winds*. Inside the cabin they flung themselves down, convulsed with laughter until the tears ran down their cheeks.

'Caspian tern,' snorted Jo.

'Marsh warbler,' giggled Jaz. 'And we thought it was drugs smugglers!'

'So the police weren't watching,' said Jo when they had eventually calmed down.

'Well, we still don't know for certain,' Jaz pointed out logically. 'One of them could have been. Or they could have been watching from a house or something. Or they could have the area bugged.'

'Yeah, or they could just be sitting comfortably in the copshop worrying about parking tickets and nicked videos,' said Jo heavily.

'Well, there's only one way to find out,' said Jaz. 'We'd better go down there and see.'

Jo hesitated. She thought of Mick and his threats. Abby was away now, safely in London, but still . . . If he found out she'd been to the police . . .

'You go,' she suggested. 'Go tomorrow. Don't mention my name.'

14

Delivery Girl

But Jaz never did get to the police station the next day.

As she got home that evening, the phone rang. Mum and Dad were closeted in the sitting-room ('Some weepy lady,' explained Alex gloomily, banished from the TV set), so Jaz answered. It was Sebastian.

'Look, I've had a great idea,' he began. 'Something's just come up—really urgent. I need to deliver some contracts to a friend of mine. Great guy, agent, knows everyone there is to know in showbiz. Well, normally I'd go myself. But with this fishing trip tonight, I'm really up to my eyes in it. Of course, I could use a courier, but then I thought of you.'

'You mean tonight?'

'No, no, tomorrow morning'll be fine. He's the ideal person for you to meet, a real expert. Knows all the shows and the TV ads, anything that's coming up where they're looking for juveniles. And I'd pay you to go. What d'you reckon—a tenner for the day? Plus expenses of course. Brilliant, eh? Helps me out and it helps you.'

'I'm not . . .'

'Look, I'd be incredibly grateful. I've just got this feeling it would be really good for you. What d'you say?'

'Oh dear, I'd like to help but . . .'

'Come on, Jasmine, be a pal.' Just for a second, Sebastian's voice lost its smooth calm. 'You'll kick yourself if you miss the opportunity. I told him I'd seen you dance, and how impressed I was. He sounded quite interested.'

Jaz faltered. 'Well, I'm not sure if . . .'

'Sorry, Jasmine, but I really must know now.'

Jaz took a deep breath. 'OK, then. Where do I go?'

'Where? Oh, it's in town.'

'Brighton?'

'No, London.'

'London!'

'No problem—train to Victoria, then get a cab. Easy. Don't tell me you couldn't manage that.'

Jaz didn't answer. She was too busy doing battle with her panic.

'Look, if you want to achieve your ambitions, you're gonna have to step out and take a few risks. Come on, Jaz, be brave.'

'OK. I'll go.'

'Great. I'll meet you at Shoreham station tomorrow morning. Nine-thirty prompt, all right? And listen, this really is a hush-hush deal. Some big names involved. So don't breath a word to anyone. OK?'

'Yes—no—all right.'

'Promise?'

'Yes, I promise.'

'Jasmine, you're a very special person. And I promise I'll do all I can to help you. See you tomorrow then. Nine-thirty.' He rang off.

What on earth had she agreed to, Jaz wondered, standing on Shoreham station the next morning. London! It was a big place. She was bound to get lost. And Mum and Dad would be furious if they knew.

But they didn't know. Mum had gone out early taking the boys by coach to visit Aunt Edie, and Dad was on the phone. Jaz had muttered something about dancing and a friend and back for tea, and escaped.

Why had she ever agreed? She'd be far too scared to say anything to this big important person. But no, I'll try, she told herself. Never pass an opportunity, Dad always said. The sort of opportunities he usually meant were spreading the gospel, but then didn't he also say, 'If God's given you a gift, you should go for it. Try and use it 100 per cent'?

And then there was the money—ten pounds! It was Mum's birthday soon, and Alex's, and spare money was hard to come by in the Walcott household.

So there she was on Shoreham Station, reading stupid adverts about Awaybreaks, just to forget the funny feeling in her stomach.

But where was Sebastian? It was 9.38 already. They'd just lowered the level-crossing gate for the approaching train when he arrived.

'Come on, I've got your ticket.' He hardly looked at her, but sped ahead on to the platform. Obediently she followed. She was surprised when he jumped on the train. She struggled to keep up with him as he pushed his way down the carriage. At the other end he stopped and pulled her into a corner outside the buffet.

'Here. Ticket—and the contracts.' He handed her a carrier bag. Inside was a large, sealed, padded envelope. 'And put this in your pocket.' He gave her a scrap of paper and three five-pound notes. 'Just ask the cab driver to take you to that address. When you get there, ask for Max.'

The whistle blew and Sebastian put his hand to the door. 'And he's got something for you to bring back. It's vital you collect it. I must have it tonight.'

There was a pause while some late arrivals climbed aboard puffing and panting.

'How were the mackerel?' asked Jaz politely, to fill in the gap.

'Mack ... oh, yes, great, caught loads. Now, don't let him forget to give you my envelope. I've got to have it.'

The guard blew the whistle again and Sebastian opened the door. 'Don't come round to my place, I won't be in. Take it home, and wait till I phone you. Don't talk to anyone else. The press would love to get their hands on some of this stuff. If anyone asks, you've come for an audition.'

'Shut the door,' yelled the guard.

'Good luck,' said Sebastian, leaping out. 'You're a good girl, I know I can trust you.'

The train jerked into motion. Jaz watched as Sebastian turned and ran from the station. She was on her own for a big adventure.

Jo was on her own and bored. She phoned Jaz, but no one was in. Everyone else she knew was away or busy. For want of anything better to do, she got on her bike and set off for the sweet shop.

As she passed Number 23, she was surprised to see the front door open. Surely Gary and his dad weren't home? She was even more surprised when

Pastor Walcott came out, carrying a sack of rubbish.

'Wotcha, Rev,' she called.

'Jodi!' His face cracked into its big beaming smile. 'You could be just the person I need. Got any spare time?'

'Too much. But what're you doing here?'

'Just having a bit of a sort-out. Ted is coming out of hospital on Monday and he's insisting on having Gary back right away. So I said I'd collect some clothes for him and I'm getting the place a bit organized while I'm here.'

'But ... Ted ... that's Mr Carter, right? He was horrible to you. He didn't like you.'

'Doesn't mean he couldn't use some help.' The Rev lobbed the rubbish into the bin. 'He was a sick man for quite a while before Jasmine found him. This place needs a good clean-up. Are you any good with a vacuum cleaner?'

Jo bumped her bike down the steps. Cleaning was not her strong point, but curiosity was. They still didn't know if this guy was the drugs dealer, and cleaning was a great way to be nosy.

That reminded her of the police station. 'Has Jaz gone out?' Jo asked over the roar of the vacuum cleaner.

'Mmm, some dance thing, she's out all day.'

'Oh,' Jo was puzzled. 'She didn't tell me.'

'Last-minute phone call, some friend from school, I think.'

Pastor Walcott was picking up endless scraps of paper from the chairs. 'D'you think these might be Gary specials?' he asked. They decided to put all the scraps in a big box. It was hard to tell what was rubbish and what wasn't with Gary around.

In the kitchen it was easier to decide. The bread had gone green and the lettuce had gone brown.

'But I still don't understand,' said Jo, scraping half-eaten remains from plates. 'How come he let you in here?'

'Well,' said the Rev, plunging his arms in the washing-up, 'I don't give up easily, you know. I reckoned it couldn't be me personally he didn't like, since he didn't really know me. So I thought I'd at least give him a chance to find out. And besides, he was desperate to see Gary and those new foster folks were too busy to take him. So I volunteered to take Gary in to visit.'

'Did he behave himself?'

'Not bad. I've picked up some tips from you on how to handle him.'

'Didn't mean Gary. I meant his dad.'

'He's OK. I reckon there's hardly anyone won't respond to a bit of warmth. The sun and the wind, you know.'

'What?'

'Don't you know the story? The sun and the wind see this man wearing a big cloak and they have a bet as to who can get it off him. The wind tries to blow it off, but the more he blows, the more the man wraps the cloak tightly round him. Then the sun starts shining, nice and gentle, and the man gets warmer and warmer and eventually he takes the cloak off by himself.'

'Yeah, but that guy's a ... Well, you should have heard the things he called Jaz. And you ... It was like he really hated you.'

'Well, now, it looked that way, didn't it? I'll admit I thought that too. But if you hang around and apply a little warmth, sometimes people start peeling off the layers, and you begin to find out what's underneath.'

He paused, dishcloth in hand. 'That man's had a lot of grief. Enough to turn anyone to hate.'

'Why? 'Cos of Gary, d'you mean?' Jaz took up a tea-towel.

'Among other things.' He paused. 'I don't think he'd mind me telling you . . . Gary wasn't always like that, you know. Up to the age of six he was quite normal—a bright kid, full of life. There was another one, a little girl of three, and his wife was expecting a third. They lived near the centre of a big city, nice house, good job. Then that summer the city erupted. There were riots. People without jobs, no-hopers, they got angry . . . It was mostly blacks.'

Jo looked up sharply, but Pastor Walcott continued, quite matter-of-fact: 'Ted was away when it happened. His wife heard the news and got scared. She decided to put the kids in the car and go to her mother's. She was driving across town when she met the joyriders—kids in a stolen car. They swung across the carriageway and came straight towards her. She swerved and they just missed, but the car went out of control. A lorry coming up behind couldn't stop.

'She was killed outright and so was the little girl. For a while it was touch and go, but Gary survived. He survived, but the doctors said he could never be the same again. Gary was brain-damaged. The joyriders never stopped and they never caught them, but witnesses said they were black.'

Jo realized she had been wiping the same plate for

several minutes. For a while the silence was broken only by the slosh of washing-up water and the rattle of cutlery.

'So I don't think Ted really hates us. He moved from the city, to make a new life for Gary. But there's all that pain locked up inside. He can only cope if he tries to forget. Then people like us turn up to remind him.'

'And Jaz crashed into him on my bike. No wonder he went mad. But how did you find all that out? Did he tell you?'

'Bit by bit. People can keep their grief locked up inside for years, and then somehow something releases it. God knows when they're ready. I was just the right person at the right time.'

Jo stacked dishes thoughtfully. This was all a bit heavy to handle.

'And as it turned out, Jasmine was the right person at the right time as well. If she hadn't turned up, he would have been a goner. I reckon that was God taking a hand, too.'

Jo handed a plate back. 'Still got food on.'

'Sorry,' said the Rev. 'Too busy talking as usual.'

What sort of sense does all this make? thought Jo. Ask God to help you fight one evil and and he sends you stumbling into another.

'But we thought . . .' she began.

'What's that?'

'Oh, nothing . . .' Now she was even more confused.

Victoria Station was noisy and confusing. People shouted when Jaz tried to get into a taxi. She turned to find a row of staring faces. They were lined up patiently behind a sign saying, 'TAXIS—QUEUE HERE'.

She crept to the back of the line.

When she did give the cabbie her piece of paper she expected him to say, 'Never 'eard of it,' or 'Don't take kids,' but he only nodded and drove off.

They drove past parks and posh shops and grand buildings with doormen in top hats and braided coats. They passed the Ritz and the Royal Academy. She recognized Picadilly Circus, a mass of lights even in the daytime. They passed theatres with photos outside and signs that said 'Sizzling sensation'——*Daily Mail* and 'Don't miss it'——*Evening Standard*.

Jaz imagined her name up there, her photo outside. She tried to picture Max's office. It would have a huge black desk and white leather sofas, she decided, with signed photos of stars all round the walls. Perhaps Max would be out at a rehearsal. 'It's just round the corner,' his secretary would say. 'Why don't you pop over there?'

At the theatre, dancers in leotards would be limbering up. Beyond the glare of the footlights, she'd find Max in the stalls, a big man with a cigar, sitting with his feet up. 'Sir,' a worried assistant would say, 'the juvenile lead's gone sick. Broken her leg.'

'Oh no, two nights till opening. That's all I need.' Then he would spot Jaz. 'Who's that pretty little lady? Say, can you dance?'

Then she would step on stage and begin her routine, nervous at first of course, but then gaining in confidence as she gave the performance of her life.

'Young lady,' Max would say, 'I think I've just found me a star.'

The taxi driver hooted and cursed a cyclist and Jaz awoke from her daydream. She found they were in a

138

narrow side street. There were still some lights and shops, but the signs said things like, 'Girls, Girls, Girls!' and 'Non-stop naughty videos'. Pungent smells wafted from the shops and Chinese traders were selling strange vegetables she'd never seen before.

The taxi turned into an even narrower street. It stopped outside a tall dingy building with barred windows.

'There you go, £7.50.'

She gave him two fivers. She had a vague feeling you should give a tip but she had no idea what it should be. She took the change. The cabbie swore at her as he drove off.

Jaz tried the black front door. It was locked. There were ten doorbells beside it. Some had names: Sadie; John Smith, aromatherapy; CTV Productions. She consulted her piece of paper: Number 6. No name beside that bell. Surely this was wrong. She looked around. The house opposite was missing, like a gap in a row of rotten teeth. Wooden props held up the boarded buildings either side. Turning back to her side of the road, she spotted a name high on the building. Shaftesbury Mansions. She checked with her piece of paper. Yes, that was right.

Could it be the next door along? She climbed the step and tripped on a pile of blankets. A voice muttered obscenities and a grey unshaven face appeared from under the dirty heap. She stepped back. Anyway that door was padlocked and there were no bells.

Reluctantly she returned and tried the bell of Number 6. The silence that followed was a relief, but she tried again, just in case. This time a grille by her left elbow made sputtering noises.

'Yes,' said a tinny voice.

'Um,' Jaz addressed the unseen voice. 'Is Max there? I've come for an audition.'

'What? Who sent you?'

'Sebastian.'

'Who? Where from?'

'Shoreham.'

'Oh, right. What's he like, this Sebastian?'

'Blond, tallish, blue eyes . . .'

'OK. Has he given you anything to deliver?'

'Um. Are you Max?'

'Yeah.'

'Yes, then. He has.'

'OK.'

A buzzer went on the door. Jaz waited.

'Come on, then. Push it,' said the voice.

Jaz pushed and found herself at the foot of a dark stairway. There were no signs or numbers, but she was aware of someone watching her from above.

'You're on your own, right?' said the same voice, less tinny and more gravelly in real life. She still couldn't see its owner.

'OK. Come up.'

As she approached the second floor she could see an open doorway. She was still aware of someone unseen watching her.

Timidly she stepped over the threshold and the door shut behind her. Someone turned the key in the lock.

'I'm Max.'

She spun round. Max was indeed fat, but it was a cigarette rather than a cigar which hung from his mouth.

'Bit young for this, aren't you? Where'd he find you?' Max didn't wait for an answer. 'Got the stuff?' He grabbed the carrier bag. 'Good. Just wait here while I check it.'

He took the bag and disappeared into a back room.

She was in an office but there were no leather sofas, no photos of stars. Just a desk, phone and typewriter, and in a corner a kettle, some mugs and a bottle of yellowing milk.

The wallpaper was faded and peeling. An ashtray overflowed with fag ends. Behind her, there was a TV set and a tired armchair. The key, she noticed, had been taken from the lock.

Max was a long time coming back. 'OK. Looks like it's all here.' He noticed her looking around. 'Yeah, temporary accommodation. Having a new office done up.'

'Sebastian said you worked on big shows,' ventured Jaz. She hadn't come this far not to say anything.

'Oh, he did, did he?'

'Do you take dancers?'

Max looked her up and down. 'You'd need to be a bit older for the sort of thing most dancers do round here.' He gave something that on a more friendly face could have been a smile.

He went to the door and replaced the key. 'OK. Thanks, kid.'

Jaz felt her body recoil with relief. She wanted to run and run and never look back, but there was still something else to get through.

'Sebastian said I was to collect something.'

'He did, huh? Yeah, I guess so. Wait here.'

He disappeared into the inner room again. Jaz just

glimpsed a bed and a phone as the door shut behind him. She waited and the fear rose once more. She must be mad. She was alone with this horrible man, with more than a passing resemblance to Jabba the Hutt, and no one knew she was here. She heard Max talking. Were there others in there? What did they really do in these half-empty seedy rooms? .

'Get out—NOW!' a voice in her head screamed.

She did, fumbling to turn the key and scrambling down the stairs in a wave of panic. She heard Max coming out behind her. 'OK doll ... What the ... ?'

She felt sure there were footsteps on the stairs behind her. She slammed the big black front door and turned left, running blindly, not looking back. The road turned the corner and ended abruptly in a row of forbidding flats. Only a narrow archway offered any possible way through.

Footsteps again—coming up behind her. Jaz ran for the brick corridor. It was dark and evil-smelling. The light at the other end proved not much help. She was in a narrow yard with huge dustbins and crates of rotting vegetables. She glanced round wildly. The yard was surrounded on two sides by the flats, on the other two by high brick walls. A silhouette appeared in the archway. She thought crazily of hiding in a dustbin. Its handles stuck out, she could at least climb on them.

Jaz had never been so glad of her gymnastic skills. With a mighty jump, she hauled herself up on a bin. From there she could see over the wall. Beyond it a narrow road clogged with traffic carried on its usual life, oblivious of the perils on her side. The bin was several feet from the wall but Jaz didn't hesitate. She leapt the gap and landed, balancing precariously. With another bound she was down on the crowded pavement and running, dodging passers-by, with tears streaming down her face.

Why had she ever come? If that guy was in show business, it certainly wasn't the sort Jaz was after. Surely Sebastian had known that. What was he doing mixed up with someone like that? Had he lied to her? She had been used, and for a moment her fear turned to anger.

Still she ran, dodging and weaving, to throw her unseen pursuer off the scent. She turned a corner and crashed into a stubble-bearded, motheaten tramp. She smelt his winey breath and heard his mumbled curses, as she tripped and fell. She picked herself up and stumbled painfully to the nearest doorway. At last she allowed herself to look round. No one was looking for her, no one was running. She was in the middle of a street market. Everyone was calmly bustling about their business: buying vegetables; examining lengths of fabric on the stalls. She began to feel foolish.

What had there been to be scared of really? Why shouldn't Max turn the key in the lock? Sebastian had warned her that it was hush-hush business. And why not a grotty office, if it was only temporary? What had Max actually done that was frightening? Nothing. It was all in her mind and now she was about to return empty-handed and Sebastian would think she was stupid.

She sank down in the doorway. She felt silly, and her ankle was hurting. In the next doorway a girl, just a few years older than Jaz, was lounging. A man, quite an old man, approached the girl. He held, Jaz noticed, a roll of fivers. Without words the girl took him inside.

Sickness returned to Jaz's stomach. She pulled herself up and was running again, unevenly on her aching ankle. All she wanted was to get out of this threatening maze of streets. She didn't care if she looked stupid, didn't care about the tenner. All she wanted was to go home.

A bus came by—a big red London bus with VICTORIA written on the front. Relieved beyond belief, Jaz jumped on.

15

True Confessions

While Jaz was enjoying the safety of a jolting London bus, Jo was rattling along in Pastor Walcott's rusty blue Vauxhall. That wasn't a particularly safe place to be, as Gary was with them—and Gary was having a bad day.

They had picked him up for a hospital visit, but between the foster home and the car he had run off down the street. When they had caught him he had banged his head and struggled to get free. Somehow Jo had managed to divert his attention and coax him into the car. Now she was holding on to him for dear life, the carrier bag of Ted's homecoming clothes wedged between her knees. He had shown her no sign of recognition, and she felt vaguely disappointed.

Before calling for Gary, they had left Number 23 clean and tidy. Jo had looked in all the cupboards and drawers she could manage, while the Pastor's back was turned. No clues, no packets of powder, nothing.

It was as she clung on, trying to stop Gary undoing the seatbelt and climbing out, that the absurdity struck her. How could you do anything top secret with Gary drawing attention to you all the time? How could anyone manage a complex drug-smuggling operation and cope with Gary's bizarre behaviour? Perhaps you could use him as a smokescreen. Jo shook her head in disbelief.

And there were other, deeper problems puzzling Jo as well. Thoughts tumbled round her head as she minded Gary in the hospital gardens, while Pastor Walcott and Ted Carter made arrangements for the homecoming. She listened for a while, intrigued at how the Pastor took Ted's prickly comments in his stride. The conversation turned to cricket and the atmosphere lightened, the two men instantly united in a passion for the game. Jo shrugged, it was a passion she didn't share. As she followed Gary's ramblings round the garden, she watched from a distance, amazed to see the two men in easy conversation, and hear the occasional snatch of laughter. The Rev, as she called him, was certainly the sort of bloke you could talk to.

After the visit, sitting in the Walcotts' kitchen, eating a very late lunch of thick slab-like cheese sandwiches, it was easy for Jo to spill out what was on her mind.

'If you believe in God, right,' she began, 'and then you see people like old Ted and all the things that've happened to him ... Well, I mean, he must be a pretty rotten God to let things like that happen to people. I mean, doesn't he care?'

'Oh yes,' said Pastor Walcott. 'He cares.'

'OK, then. Why does he let it happen?'

'To be honest, I don't know,' said the Rev thoughtfully, as he spread a thick helping of pickle over his sandwich.

Well, thought Jo as she tucked in hungrily, that's a surprise. I thought these religious types had all the answers.

'Many's the time I've struggled with that question,' continued the Rev. 'I think I'm beginning to understand some of the answers, but there are still times when I have to say, "Lord, I may not understand you, but I trust you".'

'But how can you? Trust him, I mean.'

The Rev paused for a while, as if trying to assemble the right words.

'If we were just talking about a God who was a long way away,' he began, 'who made the world, got it going and then sat back, I don't think I could trust him. But the God I believe in came to earth, lived with ordinary people, felt the sort of things I feel. So, even if I don't completely understand him, I'm pretty sure he understands me.'

'What good's understanding, if it doesn't change anything?' asked Jo.

She followed the Rev's gaze to a picture on the wall. Alex had painted it. In the awkward all-wrong drawing of a seven-year-old it showed a man with a beard holding a sort of white dog. Only you knew it was a sheep because it said 'The Good Shepherd' underneath. In the background, Alex had painted a wonky cross, with a huge shadow that stretched over the whole picture.

'When Jesus died on the cross,' continued the Rev, 'it changed everything. At first it seemed like just another rotten thing that went wrong. In a way it was. But he knew what he was doing. It was as if he drew out all the world's poison and took it into himself . . . so that in the end it could never win.'

It sounded a bit far-fetched to Jo, but it was evident the Pastor was sincere. She was silent for a while,

147

delving into a tin for a slice of Mrs Walcott's home-made banana bread.

'Didn't do much for Gary though, did it?' she asked eventually. 'Or his three-year-old sister.'

'Not if this life is all there is,' agreed the Rev. 'But what if there's more...? What if this life is just the rehearsal before the play, the pain before the birth?'

'How can you prove it?'

'I can't, but I'm staking my life on it. It'd be pretty stupid doing the job I do, if you didn't really believe what you were preaching.'

'But... it still doesn't seem fair—this life now, I mean. Some people seem to have everything—and others have sweet nothing.'

'No, it's not fair. Not now. But Jesus said some amazing things about justice. How about this? "The first shall be last." And he made it pretty clear he was rooting for the poor and the weak. I reckon it'll all get sorted out in the end.'

Wish I was that optimistic, thought Jo. She got up to put the kettle on.

But the Rev hadn't finished yet. He was just getting into his flow. 'But that doesn't mean we just sit back and let the bad side win. We're on God's side to fight injustice.'

Oh yes, the battle. Jo remembered an overheard sermon on a tired, sunshiny morning. For such a gentle easy-going bloke, he seemed really into this fighting stuff.

As if answering her thoughts, he went on, 'The thing about this battle is that we fight it the way Jesus did—with love.'

Jo was getting uncomfortable. She guessed the Rev's idea of love might be different from hers, although on reflection she wasn't too sure what hers was. But she wasn't used to conversations about love, death and judgment. It was all getting a bit too heavy. He'd be talking about sin next.

But there wasn't a next, because Mrs Walcott, Alex and Clifford returned from Aunt Edie's, chaos took over and Jo decided it was her cue to leave. They had been quite unconcerned to find her in the kitchen eating cheese sarnies and banana bread, but were surprised to find Jaz missing. 'So where's she gone?' asked Mrs Walcott. Nobody seemed very sure.

Jaz was sure of only one thing as she huddled on the train rattling its way towards Shoreham. She was very stupid to have gone into the flat of a man she didn't know, in a place she didn't know, in the middle of a busy city, when no one else knew she was there. As she thought about it, she found a piece of paper in her pocket and tore it obsessively into tiny shreds. It was Max's address, she realized. Good, she'd certainly never want that again. She tossed the shredded remains out of the window. She still couldn't figure whether Max was genuine.

Or Sebastian. Dark horrible suspicions were creeping into her mind about Sebastian. Sebastian, so open and friendly. Sebastian, who liked fitness and fresh air. She really shouldn't think bad things about people, she decided, and pushed the suspicions away. She found them reluctant to leave.

What had been in that package she was carrying? It was heavy for papers. And what was it he had wanted her to bring back? The urgency in his voice had told her it was something important.

That was another thing she was sure of. It was going to be horribly difficult to explain to Sebastian.

That evening she sat hunched on the sofa in front of the TV. Every time the phone rang, which was often in the Walcott household, she jumped nervously. And her conscience was making her miserable. Jaz didn't like lying, but she'd been completely unable to pass off her absence without inventing an elaborate alibi. It had involved a few school friends and a dance workshop in Brighton, and she had an uncomfortable feeling that sooner or later she'd have some explaining to do.

It was sooner. Not the phone call she'd expected, but the doorbell. Sebastian stood there, tanned and smiling, on the doorstep and asking Mum if Jasmine was in.

Somehow Jaz stumbled to the door and somehow she muttered an explanation and an apology for the missing package. 'I'm sorry, I just got in a panic.' Her suspicions she kept to herself.

She was aware of the fury on Sebastian's face, and his fists clenching and unclenching in frustration. She was also aware that Mum had left the kitchen door open and was keeping distant watch over her daughter and this stranger. Mum's hovering presence had its uses. He couldn't say much more than a low-voiced, 'You're useless, kid. Don't ask me to help you again,' before turning abruptly and stalking away.

'Who was that?' asked Mum from the kitchen. 'He seemed a nice young man.'

'Oh, he's a neighbour of Jo's,' Jaz improvised quickly. 'He asked me to pick up something for him in town,' (no need to mention which town) 'but I couldn't get it.'

Mum seemed satisfied with the explanation, but something was troubling her. 'I'm sure I've seen him somewhere before, but I can't think where.'

It wasn't until later when she came to Jaz's bedroom to wish her goodnight, that she remembered. 'I know where I saw him. It was at the fish market this morning. I went really early to get some for Aunt Edie—you know how she loves a fresh bit of haddock—and some bits for the cats.'

'Oh, yes,' agreed Jaz sleepily. 'He goes mackerel fishing. I 'spect he was selling his catch.'

'Mmm, it was mackerel,' Mum agreed. 'I was right behind him in the queue. But he wasn't selling them— he was buying.'

All that night Jaz tossed and turned. Why would Sebastian go out mackerel fishing and then buy mackerel? If he hadn't been catching mackerel, what had he been doing? Why had it all been so urgent that she go that morning? What had been in that package, and why was it so secret?

Low mist hung in the grey streets as Jaz set out for the Police Station. By the time she had paced up and down outside, trying to gain courage, the haze was clearing and the sun peeping through. But at last she was inside, and going hot and cold, as the man behind the desk scratched his ear in friendly deliberation.

'Smuggler, eh? I think you're letting your imagination run away with you, young lady. But even if we had been given a tip-off, I'm afraid I wouldn't be authorized to tell you.'

'Yes, but it was our tip-off. Well, sort of. Only someone else did it for us. If he did . . . But I suppose he didn't. And it was wrong anyway. At least I think so.'

The constable looked baffled and found it easiest to resort to formula. 'I'm afraid we have no authorization to give members of the public access to any information we may have received in confidence.'

'Oh . . . Oh. OK, well, thank you.' To her horror, Jaz felt her eyes begin to prickle with tears.

'Look,' the policeman lifted the counter flap, 'perhaps you'd better come in and explain exactly why you wanted to know.'

It was a relief, Jaz discovered, to unburden her fears. A policewoman came in, and then a man who flashed an identity card at her, although he wasn't in uniform. She explained everything—Mick the pusher, Mr Carter and Sebastian.

The other relief was that they took her seriously, taking notes and nodding solemnly, until at last her final and biggest worry came out in a rush.

' . . . and now it might have been me carrying drugs, and I didn't mean to, and I know you might have to arrest me, but that's all right, 'cos I've been really stupid.'

The policewoman handed her paper hankies, and a disgustingly sweet cup of tea that she was absurdly grateful to drink.

They went and got another plain-clothes man who turned out to be from Customs and Excise, and he asked her lots of questions about Sebastian's houseboat and his fishing boat and Max and where she'd been to meet him. She thought of the shredded address and realized with horror that all she remembered was 6 Shaftesbury Mansions. But they didn't seem too worried, just made her describe the journey, and then go over everything else all over again so they could record it on a tape recorder.

At the end the Customs Officer stood up and grinned cheerfully. 'Well, young lady, this may just be the break we've been looking for. We've known for ages that there's someone operating along this stretch of coast. Your Sebastian might just be the blighter we're after.'

Jaz didn't know whether to laugh or cry.

'But then again, there's absolutely no hard evidence that what you were carrying was drugs. Either way, I think you should keep well clear of this Sebastian character. He certainly sounds a bit dubious... Of course, if it turns out he is smuggling drugs, we may have to make formal charges against you as a carrier...'

Jaz gasped and tried to bite back a sob.

'... But I really don't think you'd be convicted. We're very grateful for the help you've given us. Now, would it help you if we came and talked to your parents...?'

16

Someone to Watch Over Me

'But what I don't understand,' said Mum, 'is what the mackerel have to do with it.'

'Oh Mum,' said Jaz. 'Think. If he wasn't mackerel fishing, what was he doing?'

'It's called coopering, Mrs Walcott,' explained the Customs man. 'It's a very common way for drugs to get into the country. A small boat meets a bigger ship out at sea and they pass the stuff over. We don't know if that's what he was doing, but it's quite possible.'

Mum and Dad weren't too bad once they'd got over the shock. They said she'd been very silly, but at least she'd told the truth now. All's well that ends well, they said—and then they grounded her!

Jaz wasn't surprised. She had to admit she deserved it—but later, on the phone, Jo wasn't quite so philosophical.

'Two weeks! That's a bit mean. Why'd they do that?'

The explanation put the Walcotts' phone bill up considerably, and almost left Jo speechless. 'Blimey,' she said eventually. 'Sebastian, eh? Well, I'd kind of figured we were wrong about Gary's dad.'

She was more envious than sympathetic about Jaz's

trip to London. 'Why do you get all the excitement? All I do is lurk in phone-boxes.'

'It wasn't really like that,' protested Jaz, but it occurred to her that it was quite nice to play the heroine.

'What a nerd, though.' Jo instantly deflated her pride. 'Fancy believing he was going to make you a star.'

'I didn't really,' said Jaz in a feeble voice.

'But we did, though. We were both nerds. We both believed him.'

There was a pause.

'It was obvious really,' said Jo with a sigh.

'S'pose it was,' admitted Jaz. 'I guess we just didn't want to believe it . . . I mean, he was nice.'

'Yeah, he was fun. And all that fitness and fresh air stuff.'

'And all the while he's making money out of stuff that can kill people.'

There was a silence. They both thought of Abby, but neither mentioned her name.

'I had to give your name to the police,' confessed Jaz. 'They'll probably want a statement off you. Sorry.'

'Nah, no prob, can't be helped . . . Hey, am I still allowed round to see you?'

'Well,' said Jaz truthfully, 'I think Mum sort of thought you'd got me involved in all this. Dad stuck up for you, but perhaps you'd better stay away for a couple of days until she's calmed down.'

As it turned out it was a bit longer.

The authorities didn't waste any time. For the next few days the 'twitcher' on the river bank really was watching *Shangri-La*, and the fishermen in the next boat to *Peggy Sue* were really Customs and Excise. The Customs men took Jaz up to London and drove her to two blocks called Shaftesbury Mansions. The first she didn't recognize, but the second was all too familiar, although less threatening from the safety of an anonymous car.

And then, no news.

Jaz stayed indoors, while Jo cycled past Sebastian's houseboat ten times a day, and they waited to hear of arrests.

But there were none. 'There's still no evidence,' explained a tight-lipped Customs Officer and his female sidekick as they sat drinking the Walcotts' tea a week later. They said they were from something called the Investigations Unit, which was in charge of the case from now on.

The rooms in Shaftesbury Mansions turned out to be rented by a young woman named Cindy. 'She claims she's never heard of anyone called Max.'

And Sebastian had disappeared.

'He may have suspected we were on to him, but we think not. It sounds like it's just the pattern of his behaviour to keep on the move. He may be back, and if he is, we'll be watching for him. And in the meantime we'll be trying to find out who he really is. He's certainly not an impresario called Raphael. But really there's absolutely no clear evidence that he's involved in drugs. There's nothing to prove he's more than a charming con-man.'

Jaz felt very silly.

'But what about Mick?' she queried.

'Now him we could nail down. He's definitely pushing drugs. But we're letting him hang around for the moment. You had the right idea—it's people like him who often lead us to the bigger fish.'

After the Customs Officers had gone, there were muttered conferences between Pastor and Mrs Walcott, followed by a couple of phone calls. Then they came to talk to Jaz.

They found her practising crab-walks on the weedy patch of lawn. 'Jasmine,' said Dad, 'we've arranged for you to go to Aunt Edie's for a few weeks.'

Jaz stared at their upside-down faces. 'What?'

'She'd really appreciate your help looking after Cousin Leroy.'

Jaz collapsed in an undignified heap. 'Why can't she look after her own horrible little brat? And anyway, she'll only go on at me about how dancing's the devil's work, and make me wear a hat for church, and ...'

'Jasmine.' Mum's voice rose in warning. 'It's for your own good.'

'Look, sweetheart,' explained Dad. 'You'll be safer well away from here—just till this business is sorted out. This Sebastian could be a ruthless criminal, and there's no knowing ...'

Jaz thought of Sebastian. She pictured him doing the hand jive on *Peggy Sue*, or bouncing his speedboat over the waves like a kid with a new toy. It was still hard to think of him as a ruthless criminal.

'But ...'

'If it is drugs, there could be millions of pounds involved—people do strange things for money.'

'But ...'

'No buts.' Mum and Dad went back into the house. There was evidently going to be no arguing this one.

So on Sunday afternoon, Jaz and her suitcase were

packed in the battered Vauxhall for the trip to South London, and on Monday afternoon the same Vauxhall collected Ted, Gary, a holdall and a bag full of tin cans and returned them safely home.

A few days later, there was a knock on the door of Number 23. It was Jo, holding out a plastic carton.

'Hello. Er, I made these for you an' Gary.'

Ted Carter's eyebrows lifted.

'Chocolate chip cookies. They're a bit burnt, but not that much.'

The eyebrows lowered. 'Oh, it's you. I can manage, you know. I don't need charity.'

'Who said you did? I was only being friendly.'

There was a silence while Jo hovered, uncertain, on the doorstep. Mr Carter lifted the lid and stared at the misshapen offerings. He made a big effort and said they looked very nice. Gary, who had come up behind him, said nothing, but grabbed a handful of biscuits and started eating and that said it all.

Still Jo hovered.

'Did you want to come in?'

It was hardly a warm invitation but Jo stepped inside and shuffled uncomfortably from foot to foot.

'They're to say sorry, you see, 'cos me and Jaz thought you were a drugs smuggler.'

Ted Carter sat down heavily. 'No, I'm afraid I don't see.' He was a big man with a red face and they'd just spent a lot of time in the hospital telling him that chocolate chip cookies were exactly the sort of thing he shouldn't eat, but he nibbled one anyway, as Jo launched into her explanation.

'It was *Mary Jane* that confused us. It means

marijuana, see? We thought it was a sort of code.'

Mr Carter smiled, a sad sort of smile. He glanced at a photo on the mantlepiece. 'Catherine Mary Jane—my wife. I named the boat after her. We'd only just got it when ...'

'The Rev told me ... I hope you don't mind?'

'Great, let the whole world know my affairs. Let's have the whole of Shoreham feeling sorry for me.'

'He only told me to explain why you were so ... I mean why you weren't really ... I mean ... to help me understand.'

'Yes, yes, all right, I get the picture... Anyway, *Mary Jane* is nothing more than a boat.' He got up out of the armchair, glancing at Gary who was absorbed in cartoons. 'Come on, then. Have a look. Prove I'm not inventing it.'

He led the way out to a garage facing the access road at the back. He lifted the door. There was Mary Jane, a neat little sailing dinghy. 'I kept it in memory of her. Couldn't bear to sail it, or part with it, either. When we came here I thought perhaps I'd go sailing again. But somehow I never got round to it. It's got an outboard. Cathy was never quite convinced of my sailing skills.'

He stared at it silently for a moment.

Jo didn't know what to say. 'It's lovely,' she said awkwardly. 'Tell you what. If you want to take it out, I'll look after Gary for you.'

He looked at her thoughtfully as he shut the garage door. 'I could almost be tempted to take you up on that.'

They had left Gary in front of the TV. When they returned the room was empty. 'Oh no,' said Mr Carter wearily.

'He didn't go out. We'd have seen 'im.'

'He's probably upstairs.'

'Rest yer ticker, I'll go.'

Gary was in his room, staring out of the window. A row of tin cans and foil-covered containers were arranged across his window sill. He had taken the chocolate chip cookies with him—and a can of coke, shaken then opened, by the looks of the sticky trail across the carpet.

Mr Carter had followed her upstairs. Silently and wearily he found a cloth and between them they cleared up the mess.

'How ever d'you manage?' asked Jo, scooping up biscuit crumbs. 'You can't even turn yer back.'

'It wasn't so bad when he was at the special school,' explained Mr Carter. 'They did so much for him there, but then it closed—cutbacks, you know. They found him somewhere else but it just wasn't suitable. He was so unhappy and frustrated that in the end I kept him home. Gave up work so I could be with him.'

'You mean you're on your own with Gary all day long? Don't you go spare?'

'Sometimes—but there doesn't seem a lot of choice. He needs a residential place, really, but they just haven't come up with one. I've tried to look myself, but with him around, how can I do it? It's just too much.'

'If I looked after him now and then, would it help?'

'You're too young. I couldn't give you the responsibility. It'd be too much for someone your age.'

'No one ever thinks I can manage anything. Makes me sick. Jaz an' me managed, didn't we? Ask the Rev.'

'I'm not asking for help.'

160

'Don't see why not. Are ya too proud or what?'

'Look, I've had offers of help before. People start off well, but when they discover what it's really like, they disappear into the mist.'

'I like Gary,' protested Jo. She was surprised at herself for saying it, but it was true. 'Can't you trust nobody?'

Ted Carter paused, mopping-up cloth in hand. 'I suppose I've got out of the habit. You're OK with Gary, better than most, and . . .' the words came out in a rush, 'I appreciate your kindness, but you're still far too young.'

'I'm always too young, or too irresponsible, or too thick . . .' Jo muttered to herself as she clattered down the wooden stairs and headed for home.

But Ted Carter did ask the Rev, and he suggested that Jo bring Gary to the holiday play scheme at the chapel each afternoon. 'We couldn't manage him on our own, but if Jo's responsible for him, and there are other adults around, it'll give you a break. Are you sure you're not just too proud to ask for help?'

'People keep asking me that,' said Mr Carter. 'OK. God knows, I need a break.'

'Yup,' muttered Pastor Walcott as he put down the phone. 'I reckon he does.'

And so the days went by. Jaz sent a couple of bored postcards from Catford, and each afternoon, Jo collected Gary and took him down to the holiday club. Abby was safe at Dad's, and no one mentioned drugs or smugglers.

It was eleven o'clock on Bank Holiday Monday, and Jo was just getting up. Mum was sitting at the table in her dressing-gown, making fiddly earrings out of wire and beads. Outside, iron-grey clouds scudded across the sky and the odd raindrop crashed against the cabin window.

'There's nothing worse,' observed Jo, 'than a rainy Bank Holiday with nothing to do.'

Mum considered. 'No, sunny ones with nothing to do are worse. At least if it's raining you can feel sorry for all the poor devils who thought they were going to have a wonderful time. Anyway, there is something to do. Your father's coming to take you out.'

'Oh, with Abby?'

'How should I know?'

Dad breezed in at lunch-time, and guarded tension filled the cabin.

'Abby?' he echoed, surprised, when Jo asked him. 'No, she left me weeks ago. It only took a few days for her to get fed up with my company. She was like a cat on hot bricks. I think the break-in finished her off.'

'Break-in? What break-in?'

'It was just after I'd been paid cash for my last gig. They took all that, and the stereo. I suppose we were asking for it, with the window left open. Just my luck. I never usually keep cash in the house. It was Abby's fault about the window. She admitted it, but I think it upset her.'

'Where'd she go?'

'Back to her flat, I suppose. Haven't you seen her?'

A chill passed through Jo's body. She reached for the phone and dialled Abby's number. It rang long and insistently. Jo held on, stubbornly listening to each empty ring and willing someone to answer.

'I should think she's gone away. You know your

sister, some hare-brained scheme,' said Dad, peering out at the rain.

'It is summer, Jo. She's probably waitressing, or chambermaiding,' said Mum.

'But why hasn't she said?' Jo's stomach was churning.

'Jo, she's nearly twenty-one. Old enough to run her own life. She doesn't have to tell us everything... Still,' Mum mused, 'it's not like her not to pop round.'

'The girls are growing up, Maggie,' said Dad. 'You have to let them go their own ways.'

'Like you do, you mean?'

Dad decided to change the subject. 'Hey Jo, the new Spielberg film's on in Brighton, and there's that burger place with the Sixties music we were going to try.'

'Yeah, fine,' said Jo dully. 'Let's go.'

It was like most days out with Dad—unsatisfactory. He fired a lot of questions at her and got irritable if she didn't want to answer. But if she did answer it was never good enough.

'You ought to be going out and having fun, not looking after that stupid handicapped kid... Don't know why I bought that saxophone, if you're never going to play it... Why d'you keep worrying about Abby? If you do half as well as her you'll be doing fine.'

The film was quite funny, but they laughed more than it deserved. The burger bar was too loud for talk, but that was a help. Neither activity took as long as they expected and then there was nothing to do.

'How about ten-pin bowling?' asked Dad. He was trying to be nice. 'No thanks, Dad. It's been a terrific day, but there's this party tonight.' (There was a party—somewhere there must be. Jo wasn't going to it, but who said she was?)

'Hey, that's my girl.' Dad sounded relieved. 'Getting too old to want her Dad around these days.'

'Just as well,' thought Jo, grumpily. 'Chance'd be a fine thing.'

He dropped her back home at the end of the footpath, with jovial promises to be back soon.

Am I, she wondered vaguely, getting too old to want my Dad? She put the thought to one side. There was another question pounding through her head, one that wouldn't go away.

Whatever's happened to Abby?

17

Stand by Me

All that week Jo phoned Abby's flat. The hollow ringing echoed her fears. She phoned several times each day, and even checked with the operator. Then the following Monday it was answered.

Mel was back from holiday. 'Oh hi, Jo. Hang on . . . No sorry, she's out . . . Don't know. She's out a lot. Try in a few days.'

Jo tried in a few days, and a few days more, and Abby was always out.

'Is she all right, Mel?' she asked desperately.

'Fine,' said Mel, uncertainly. 'Yeah, she's OK. Look, I'll make sure she phones you some time. Don't worry.'

But Jo did. Term had started by now and suddenly GCSEs were a reality instead of a threat. Everyone was lecturing her about the importance of the next two years, and she did want to try, honest she did, but she stared into space, doodled on her textbooks, 'lost' her homework and her mind was far away.

Jaz, back from her exile with Aunt Edie, tried to sympathize, but it seemed that nothing she could say was right.

'How do you know what it's like?' Jo would retort.

'All your family are so holy and nice. You've never been through it. You don't know what it's like in the real world.'

'And I don't,' Jaz complained to her mother, as she watched her stirring a big fish stew. 'But I can't suddenly make my life different. I don't know what to say. I've tried to tell her that Jesus loves her and that I'm praying for her, but it just makes her cross. I feel so useless.'

'Give this a stir, while I do the rice,' said Mum. 'She hasn't stopped talking to you, has she?'

'No, she comes and tells me the same worries over and over. But I don't know what to say.'

'It doesn't matter. It doesn't really matter what you say. There's some people have got the gift of the gab, like your Dad. And there's others—you and me—who can't string half a dozen words together without getting in a tangle. But what matters most is to listen. Usually that's the most valuable gift you can give anyone.'

It was a long speech for Mum. She was best at just quietly getting on and doing things for people—and she was good at listening, Jaz realized—although these things often went unnoticed.

'Just listen,' repeated Mum, straining water off the rice, 'and be around when people need you. That's what matters most.'

So Jaz listened and Jo talked, going round and round in circles until she finally resolved to go into Brighton at the weekend.

'Jaz,' she asked awkwardly on Friday morning. 'I know this is a bit chicken, but will you come with me? Maybe not as far as visiting Abby, but at least come with me on the bus.'

'Course,' said Jaz. 'Course I'll come.'

But on Friday lunchtime a buzz went round the school. Someone brought in a local paper and there on one of the back pages was an ad.

WANTED FOR NEW TV SERIES
Girls aged 13–16
Lively and attractive with good dancing skills
Are you the one we're looking for?
Come to an audition at Glenlea Ballroom
Saturday 8 Sept 10 a.m.

'No, you go,' said Jo. 'Honest, it's a great chance, don't miss it. Tell you what, I needn't go till the afternoon. How about if we meet by the Palace Pier at two o'clock? You're bound to have finished by then.'

By ten o'clock on Saturday morning a queue of young hopefuls stretched out of the Glenlea Ballroom and round the block. Jaz arrived at 9.45. Clearly all the old hands had turned up hours earlier.

A bored girl with orangey-green hair took their details. Anyone without dance qualifications was weeded out immediately. Nervously Jaz quoted her gold medal for gym and her dance school certificates.

'Yep,' said Orange-Hair. 'Next.'

Jaz stood there uncertainly. 'Go on,' said the girl brusquely, 'You're in.'

The ballroom was packed with lithe bodies in shiny lycra. Jaz, in her school regulation leotard, thought they all looked terribly smart and sophisticated. Some looked thirteen going on twenty-one, although a few looked twenty-one trying terribly hard to look thirteen.

Eventually a tiny woman dressed in black came and stood centre floor. A hush fell.

'We'll be taking you in groups of eight. Just come out when your name's called and follow the routine I give you,' she said briskly.

Jaz sat in a corner concentrating hard, as they did the same routine over and over again. Desperately she ran over it in her head. She knew she could do it. Group after group went on. Most were sent away. Occasionally someone was picked out. She looked at her watch. 1.30.

'Call me next,' she willed. 'I might still make it.'

They didn't. Name after name was called. 1.50 and sixteen people still remained. Any minute now Jo would be waiting by the pier. 'I promised,' thought Jaz, '. . . but Jo'd understand. She'd want me to go for it.'

Minutes ticked by. 'I can't let her down,' thought Jaz, and then, 'I can't give up the chance.'

Indecision has a way of making decisions for you. It was 2.09. 'Too late anyway,' thought Jaz.

'Jasmine Walcott,' called Orange-Hair.

Jo stood on Abby's crumbling doorstep and pressed the bell until her finger hurt. She didn't care. She was going to hold it there till someone answered.

Someone did. Dragging footsteps sounded on the stairs and at last the door swung open. Abby stood there—alive at least—but the picture of Jo's worst fears.

Her eyes, once bright and dancing, were blank and hollow. Her skin was dull and blotchy, her clothes stained. No outrageous make-up, no flamboyant colours.

'Oh, sis. Look, come round some other time. Please. I'm not feeling too good. Sorry.'

She went to shut the door. Jo pushed it back again. She prepared to use all her strength, but it didn't need much.

'Sorry or not, I'm coming in.'

She shut the door behind her and pushed Abby back up the stairs, half-angry, half-scared, but wholly determined.

In the sitting-room she shoved Abby into a chair and sat down opposite. The two sisters regarded each other in appalled silence.

A heavy smell hung over the room—stale tobacco, unwashed clothes. The room was a mess—that was nothing unusual—but it was a sad, dingy mess, not the usual full-of-life mess of parties and paintings. Matches and scraps of tin foil littered the floor by Abby's chair. The curtains were closed.

Abby's eyes looked like that, thought Jo. Windows with tightly-closed curtains.

All Abby saw was the look of shock on her sister's face. 'Look kid, it's OK. Touch of flu, that's all. Knocked me back a bit.'

'It's not OK and it's not all. And I'm not a kid. I don't know what stupid stuff you're taking, but I can see what it's doing to you. I want you alive, not dead like Dimitri who tried to fly.'

'How d'you know about Dimitri?'

'I just do.'

A spark of fight came into Abby's face. 'Jo, it's this stuff that's keeping me alive. I wouldn't have coped, all through the degree show and everything, without it. It's got a bit on top of me right now, but I'll shake it off.'

'You do want to, then?'

Abby scratched her arms and fidgeted restlessly. 'Course.'

'Have you been to the doctor's or anything?'

'No, they wouldn't help, and anyway I can't. I've got a place for graduate studies. It's a brilliant chance. If the college find out, I've blown it.'

'They needn't know.'

'I'm not taking the risk.'

'Tell Mum or Dad. They'll help.'

'Oh come on, be real! Mum'll shout and scream and Dad won't want to know.'

'But there must be clinics or something. I know this Reverend bloke. He might find you something.'

'Look, I don't want religion, I don't want doctors, I don't want Mum, or Dad—or you—breathing down my neck. I just want space. I just want a chance to sort things out my way.'

Abby sat hunched, running her hands endlessly round her tangled hair.

'Please, don't tell Mum or Dad. Trust me, I've always managed before. I'll kick it. Just give me space. Please don't tell anyone. Promise you won't.'

Jo looked miserable and doubtful.

'Come on, Jo. We've always stuck together, haven't we? Promise? Promise.'

'All right.'

Abby sighed and leaned her head on her arms.

'Life's just too stinking hard. You're only a kid. You don't understand how hard it is.'

'But ... but you ... It's always been so easy for you. You've always been good at everything. You've always had friends.'

Abby looked up. 'On the surface, maybe. It's different underneath.'

The words hung in the fetid air. Jo sat helpless, the promise like a heavy weight round her neck.

The sound of the doorbell punctured the long silence. Three short rings. Abby stirred herself and went to the window. She raised it and peered out.

'Hang on, I'm coming down,' she shouted.

Abby delved into a cupboard and pulled something out. Jo listened till the footsteps reached the bottom of the stairs. Then she tiptoed out and leant over the landing. There was some sort of transaction going on in the dark hallway. Abby had closed the front door behind the two callers, and they were speaking in hushed tones. But when she let them out and returned upstairs, she was counting ten pound notes.

'You're pushing!' Jo stood angry and accusing at the head of the stairs.

'It's not like that. They're my mates. We help each other out.'

'They were only kids.'

'They're sixth-formers. How else d'you suppose I get enough money?'

'I know how else! Stealing. Nicking stuff from yer own Mum and Dad.'

'Listen, even if I nicked everything they had, it wouldn't be enough. Do you know how much it costs? This stuff sells at about £100 a gram. There are other ways to get money, but...'

'I'm telling!' Jo clattered down the stairs and past her sister. 'I don't care if it's the college, or Mum and Dad, or even the police. It's one thing to ruin yer own life...'

Abby whirled round to face her. 'Go on, then. Go ahead. It'll be you ruining my life, if you do. Stop my career, get me a prison sentence. What for? To make you feel good? To spite big sister? Nothing like interfering in other people's problems to make you feel better about your own.'

'You are my problem,' whispered Jo as she let herself out of the door.

'Tomorrow morning—ten-thirty—for the final selection. Is that a problem for anyone?'

The woman dressed in black looked round at the twenty remaining hopefuls. Jaz felt her heart start thumping and her head spinning. When she had been picked she had thought that was it. But the woman explained that only five were needed. Tomorrow they were going to test them on camera—and then make the final choice. With churning stomach, Jaz remembered how she'd made all that fuss about going to church instead of the gym display. She had to stand by it now. She wanted to, but ...

'No problem,' she heard herself agreeing.

'God understands,' she muttered to herself as she left the ballroom. 'I don't know about Mum and Dad, though.'

'She's not back from the audition,' said Mrs Walcott when Jo knocked on the door. 'Been gone hours.' She noticed Jo's red-rimmed eyes. 'But come in, love. Have a cup of tea.'

'No, no, I'll come back later.'

Jo turned wearily back down the path. Mrs Walcott watched her go. Jo wasn't a bad kid. She didn't know what was wrong but she wished she could help.

A few hundred metres down the road was the old chapel. The door was open, Jo noticed through blurry eyes.

She peered inside. Dust hung in shafts of sunlight. Old worn Bibles sat neatly at the pew ends. A bunch of flowers stood in a bucket—ready for tomorrow, she supposed. But there were no signs of life.

She slipped into the back pew. It was solid, polished, comforting. How many people had sat here and prayed over the years? Had they ever felt as desperate as she did? She stared up at the shimmering flecks of dust.

'God,' she whispered into the silence, 'now what do I do?'

Pastor Walcott, bustling out of the vestry with an armful of church notice-sheets, paused at the sight of the figure slumped in the back pew.

'Jodi, welcome to church. Nice and early. Wrong day, though.'

She managed half a smile. 'That's me. I get most things wrong.'

'Oh dear. Such as?' He came and sat across the aisle, stuffing notice-sheets into hymnbooks and building a neat pile.

'If you had someone,' began Jo slowly, 'someone special, like in your family, and you knew they were doing something stupid, something wrong—would you tell on them? I mean, if they'd made you promise not to?'

The Rev looked at her thoughtfully. 'Now that depends. It depends on a lot of things. Would you like to tell me about it?'

Yes, I would, thought Jo, but I can't.

'No, not really,' she said. 'It's no big deal. I just wondered. Like if you knew that person trusted you, and if you told, you'd let them down and they'd never like you again.'

'Sometimes telling the truth is more important than people liking you. Sometimes you have to do hard things for people, because you love them. Like smacking Clifford when he goes too near the fire.'

'Or sending Jaz to Aunt Edie's?'

The Rev smiled. 'Mmm, like that.'

'But if it spoilt things for them if you told? Or if it meant breaking a promise? And what if you promised, and then you found out that what they were doing was worse than what you promised you wouldn't say?'

'Now that sounds complicated.' The Rev straightened his pile of books while he thought. 'Some things are complicated though. Sometimes there are just no easy answers. Tell you what I do at times like that, when I've thought and thought and I just can't figure it out. I pray.'

'I've tried that. Sort of.'

'Well then, let God sort it out. He will. Just keep listening for his answer. It may not always be the way you expect it, but I've found one usually comes.'

'I have prayed about it,' said Jaz defiantly. 'It's the chance of a lifetime.'

'Look love, you know what we think,' said Mrs Walcott. 'And the truth is, we're not happy about it. But we've decided it's up to you.'

'There were hundreds going for it, hundreds, and I'm in the last twenty. I've got to go when they say. I've got to go! I'll never get a chance like it again.'

'It's up to you.'

'Oh.'

'You're old enough to decide what's most important in your life,' agreed Pastor Walcott, disappearing into his tiny study with a sheaf of sermon notes. 'We're not going to make you come to church. You have to decide for yourself.'

'Oh . . . Right.'

'By the way,' said Mum. 'Jo called round. She seemed a bit upset.'

'Go back to the flat. Go back to the flat.' The words were pounding round Jo's head as she crossed the footbridge home. She wasn't sure where they'd come from, but she wasn't very convinced.

'Look God,' she argued. 'If I go back, she won't let me in. What's the point? She wouldn't let me in if I paid her. Well, she might if I paid her, she certainly wouldn't otherwise.'

'Abby phoned,' Mum said when Jo got back to *Trade Winds*. 'She's had flu apparently, really badly. That's why she hasn't been in touch. She says you were upset because she looked so ill. That's why she phoned. She didn't want you coming back upsetting me. She can be a thoughtful girl sometimes.'

Mum put the kettle on and spooned coffee into a cup. 'She says you got the wrong end of the stick entirely. Thought she'd been on drugs, when all it was was antibiotics. Really Jo, you are fanciful sometimes. D'you want a cuppa?'

'What? Oh, no thanks.' Jo was stunned into silence.

'Anyway, she's got Mel there now,' Mum continued, 'and she's feeling lots better. But listen, I was thinking. Why don't you go back to the flat tomorrow and take her some money? She's broke, of course. Well, she couldn't get a holiday job. I'd go over myself, but it's the Worthing Craft Fair—one of my few chances to make some money. You could take some groceries for her, as well. And why don't you make her some of your chocolate chip cookies?'

'No, really, no sweat.' said Jo into the phone. 'Course you couldn't make it. Twenty out of five hundred, that's brilliant.' She tried incredibly hard to be cheerful. 'I'm OK, honest. Anyway, I'm going back. Tomorrow morning. I know you can't come what with the audition and church and everything. It'll be all right. I can cope.'

That night Jaz discussed Sunday morning options with God. What if I went to church first, then to the audition and then went with Jo? What if I went with Jo really early, then popped in to the audition and said I'd be back later, then went to church? What if . . . ?

It was no good, she had to make a choice.

18

Bad Trip

The next morning Jo was awakened by a phone call.

'It's Jaz. I've decided I'll come with you.'

So, with a bag of groceries, an envelope of bank notes and her friend at her side, Jo set out for Brighton once more. As they passed the Glenlea Ballroom they could hear music inside.

'Isn't that your thing on now?' asked Jo.

'No, I can pop in later.' Jaz's step didn't falter. 'I'll come with you.'

Jo was unusually quiet as they plodded up the hill. As they reached Abby's doorstep she paused.

'I'm all right on me own now. You go to your audition.'

'But I decided to come with you.'

'No, it's between me and Abby. I've decided.'

'You mean you don't really want me anyway?'

'Nah, course I don't. Go on. I'll come and meet you there.' Jo's anxiety made her sound much crosser than she meant. 'It's my problem, nothing to do with you. Go on!'

She stood on the doorstep and watched as Jaz ran

back down the steep street. Then she rang the bell.

It was a different person doing the audition this time, a tall man in a baseball cap who looked puzzled when Jaz came panting up to him.

'No, we've finished. But you weren't on the list.'

'Yes, I was. There, Jasmine Walcott.'

'Give me strength! These choreographers, they just don't listen. Don't worry. You didn't miss anything. I specifically asked for white kids.'

Jaz turned away, stunned. She'd tried to make the right choices and they'd turned round and slapped her in the face. Disappointment boiled up into anger.

She came back and stood over the man in the baseball cap. He was kneeling on the floor stuffing papers in a leather satchel. She took a deep breath.

'That's not fair. You're not allowed to do that. There's supposed to be equal opportunities. You can't turn me away because of the colour of my skin.'

The man straightened and stood up till he was looking down on her from what seemed a very great height. He took off his cap and rumpled his hair, then smiled in amusement.

'You've got a nerve. Turn up late, burst in, and then tell the director what he mustn't do. Feisty young madam!'

'I . . . Oh . . . I didn't . . .'

'OK, just for your cheek . . .' He took a cassette and thrust it into a recorder. 'Go on, you've got one minute to convince me.'

The tune was unfamiliar. Jaz, still out of breath from her run and trembling from her outburst, kicked off her shoes, stumbled to the centre of the floor and managed as best she could. But she didn't even last the minute. Her foot caught on something as she went into a somersault. It was only a piece of paper, but enough to send her falling awkwardly to the floor.

'OK, OK.' He turned the tape off abruptly. 'That wasn't really a fair trial. You've got the beginnings of a nice style there, though, and good looks too. But they'd stick out in this production, I'm afraid.'

Jaz was silent, bending down to replace her shoes.

'Look, didn't they tell you? The series is set in the 1920s. How many black faces do you think there were in Brighton seventy years ago?'

'Oh . . . I . . . Oh . . . Not many.'

The man swung his satchel over his shoulder. 'Joke is, it's called "The Good Old Days". Not so good, eh?' He delved into his pocket. 'Here.'

He handed her a card. 'Movers and Shakers,' she read, 'multi-cultural youth dance workshop.'

'Friend of mine runs it. Mention my name.'

She looked up questioning.

'Oh, Anton Shebinsky,' he said, picking up the cassette player. He smiled at her, with tired brown eyes surrounded by crinkly lines. 'There's plenty of disappointments in this game, Jasmine Walcott. Don't give up. Hang on in there.'

Again Jo faced the sickening wait as the bell rang distantly in the upper flat. She hung on. This time Mel answered.

She looked frightened. 'Oh, Jo. It's not very convenient right now.'

'I've got some money from Mum.'

'That's nice. I'll give it to her.'

'No, I want to see her.'

'Well, I'm not sure.'

'Mum gave me some messages and they need an answer. I can't give her the money otherwise.'

'Oh . . . Hang on, then. I'll see.'

Jo waited. Mel took a long time to return. Her gentle round face was furrowed with anxiety. 'Look, she's really not very well today.'

'I've got to see her.' Jo pushed past Mel and slammed up the stairs. She didn't know what she was going to do, or why it was so important, but if that voice in her head was God she supposed she'd better do it.

Jo dashed in panic around the flat. Abby wasn't in the sitting-room, or the kitchen. She was in the bedroom, spreadeagled across the bed. Her eyes stared glassily at the ceiling, her mouth was open. Every so often she twitched convulsively. The room smelt of sick. 'Abby, what is it? Abby, can you hear me?'

Abby groaned and retched.

Mel appeared in the doorway, white and scared.

'Mel, what is it? She's really ill. What's up?'

'Jo, I don't know, honest.'

'Is this what drugs do? Why would anyone put themselves through that?'

Mel looked guilty and confused. 'No, it's not what normally happens.' She tried to pull Jo from the room. 'Leave her, she'll be OK soon.'

'No, no, she could choke like that.'

First Aid lectures from school came tumbling into Jo's mind. Couldn't people choke on their own vomit? Didn't you have to put them . . . ? How did you put them? She wished she'd listened properly. It was something like—on their front . . . head on one side ... make sure they can breathe. Desperately she tried to turn Abby. She flopped over like a half-empty bean bag.

'I think,' ventured Mel, 'I think someone sold her some bum smack.'

'Some ...?'

'Heroin ... It's what she's ... It's what we're ... Somebody sold her dirty stuff. It's got something in it making her like this.'

'Have you called a doctor?'

'No. She wouldn't want that, I know she wouldn't. It'll pass, honest.'

Abby groaned and tried to push herself up. Jo found herself the focus of her sister's sweating, hollow-eyed gaze.

'Well, I'm not gonna wait to find out. I'm going to call a doc.'

Jo marched out to the phone with greater determination than she felt. She picked up the receiver, then paused. Who did she phone? Her doctor in Shoreham? Was there a college doctor? Dial 999? Should she do that? Perhaps Mel was right and it would pass and she'd look really silly.

A commotion from the bedroom interrupted her panic. Abby was stumbling out, half-held back, half-supported by Mel.

'What? What're you doing kid? Mind yer own ...' Abby lunged at Jo and tried to catch the phone.

And then Jo was screaming: 'You stupid idiot, I don't care who I tell.' She punched at the nines on the phone with quivering fingers.

And Abby was running, half-falling, down the stairs and onto the street. And Mel was following, then Jo, and there was a screech of brakes and a dull thud, and then silence, and a tiny voice on a dangling phone saying, 'Hello caller, which service do you require?'

Once more Jo was hospital visiting. The ward was hushed. Mum and Dad sat, together for once, beside the bed. The figure they were watching lay motionless.

But Abby was breathing, peacefully and rhythmically, and it was all going to be all right.

It hadn't seemed like that at first. When Jo had rushed out into the street and seen the blood on the car's bonnet and Abby's limp body tossed onto the ground, her whole world seemed as shattered as the car's windscreen.

'If it had been going even five miles per hour faster,' said the doctor, 'it would have been a different story.'

But as it was, there were cuts and bruises, a broken collar-bone, and still the effects of the evil powder, making its poisonous way through her system.

In the end, Jo never had to tell. Mel, shocked and weeping, had said it all anyway. The hospital had contacted Mum and Dad and they'd come together, in an unspoken truce, to sit united in fear and guilt at Abby's side in the Casualty department.

'It's all going to be all right,' thought Jo. The worst was over.

Dad had come back to the houseboat after that first traumatic evening, and he and Mum had talked long into the night. At first their voices had been raised and angry, blaming each other, and Jo had buried her head in the pillow, not wanting to hear.

But gradually they had quietened. She'd heard Mum sobbing, maybe Dad too, and drifted off to sleep to the rhythmic rise and fall of their voices. And in the morning, Dad had still been there. He'd been down the baker's really early and Jo woke to the smell of hot bread rolls and fresh coffee, just like it used to be. And even more like it used to be—a very long time ago— he and Mum were friends, teasing each other with a sort of sad tenderness.

So here they were, waiting for Abby to wake up, and Jo couldn't suppress the little bubbles that kept rising to the surface of her mind—bubbles of hope.

Abby opened her eyes. Full of emptiness. It was a silly expression they'd used when they were kids, but that's what came to Jo's mind. Abby managed a smile. 'Hi Mum, sorry to be such a nuisance . . . Oh, Dad, hi.' She looked nervous and guilty.

'You're not a nuisance.' Dad was being uncommonly bright and positive. 'It's just a bad patch. You're tough, you'll pull through.'

Abby closed her eyes and turned her head away. She opened them again and saw Jo. 'You told them, you broke your promise.'

'You mean you knew?' Dad broke in before Jo had a chance to protest. 'You knew about the drugs and you kept it secret? Why? You're not on them too?'

'Course not.' Mum sprung to her defence, then wavered. 'Are you?'

'No, I'm not!'

'She'd better not be,' Abby's weary voice chipped in. 'She went on at me enough times.'

'Why didn't you tell us?' The question was addressed both to Abby and Jo, but neither answered.

'What went wrong?' asked Dad. 'You were always so confident, so good at everything.'

'That's what you thought!' said Abby. 'That's what you wanted to think. Everyone did. No one asked how I really felt. So I just kept trying. It got harder and harder. I knew one day I'd blow it.'

'But why drugs?' asked Mum.

'They were around. It was easy. For a while it was cocaine. That kept me going, gave me a lift. Then I got on to heroin. It made me feel warm and easy, like I didn't have to try any more. I suppose it was a sort of escape.'

'Water under the bridge,' said Mum. 'The important thing now is to get better. Why don't you come home to live?'

'On the boat? There's hardly room for the two of you.'

'Or come back to me,' put in Dad, a hint of the old battle creeping in.

'With you?' Abby's voice raised above a monotone. 'You and Alison?'

'Who's Alison?' asked Jo.

'His bimbo,' said Abby.

'I was going to tell you,' said Dad, looking at the floor.

Mum said nothing.

Jo sat silent, hopes dashed. Mum and Dad sat tensely on their separate chairs, the gap between widened to a chasm.

'Anyhow,' said Dad, 'it's Abby we're concerned about at the moment.'

'Typical—change the subject,' muttered Mum.

'The hospital social worker gave us details of a drugs clinic you can go to. It's expensive, but we'll pay. If you want to.'

'Yes, I do, I do want to.' Abby's eyes filled with tears. 'D'you think I meant to get like this? But you don't know it all.'

She began a catalogue—Mum's ring, Dad's stereo, £100 here, £500 there. When she'd finished the tears were streaming down her face—and Mum's, and Jo's, and even Dad's. He had started angrily as he realized the 'break-in' at his flat was Abby's work. But now he was quietly wiping his nose.

When the list stopped there was silence.

'You're still my daughter,' said Mum.

'And mine,' said Dad.

'It's gonna be all right,' thought Jo. 'It's not too late.'

Late that night Mum and Jo, alone on *Trade Winds*, sat with hands wrapped round mugs of hot chocolate. In the corner the TV churned out endless words and images: make-believe lives, other people's lives, all safely contained in a box. It was no more than moving wallpaper to Jo and Maggie Thomas, absorbed in the real drama in their heads.

'It wouldn't have worked,' said Mum suddenly. 'Dad and me. I know you wanted it.'

'Not now he's got a girlfriend.'

'It's not just Alison. Good luck to her, I say. I'd already told him I was going ahead with the divorce. I'm sorry if you mind, but honestly, it's a great big relief. And now I don't have to be married to him, I actually feel we can be friends . . . Sorry.'

'No sweat, Mum.' Jo fumbled for words. 'Water under the bridge. We'll be all right, Abby, you and me.'

But the next day when they came to collect Abby,

her bed was empty. A bored-looking nurse handed them a note. 'Discharged herself. Left this.'

Dear Mum and Dad and Jo,

Sorry for all the hassle I've put you through. I know things need to change, but it's just not that easy. I can't do it overnight. I need to work this out for myself, and I need some space. I've gone away for a while. Don't try and find me.

Love you,
Abby

19

We Are Sailing

'Just because the person goes away, it doesn't mean the pain does,' said Jo.

'I know,' Ted Carter agreed quietly.

They were in the garage fiddling with ropes and sails.

'It never quite goes away,' said Ted, 'but it gets easier. There are more and more good days, until one day you wake up and discover you're actually feeling happy. Like this morning.'

The day had finally come. The grand launch of *Mary Jane*. They had talked about it on and off for weeks.

'When ya gonna take that boat out then, Mr Carter?' Jo had asked each day as she brought Gary back from the play scheme.

'One day,' he'd reply. 'Soon.'

But the 'one day's and 'soon's came and went and he started finding excuses: 'the weather', 'the tides', 'heart's a bit dicky today', 'Gary's being difficult'. Jo came to realize that there were other reasons that meant Ted Carter wasn't yet ready to sail his boat.

So she stopped asking, although she couldn't resist the occasional hint. He smiled a bit these days, and had told Jo to call him Ted. He started talking to the neighbours, even went for drinks with Charlie Finn, and sometimes on Sundays took Gary down to the little chapel.

But today, a glorious Saturday in late September, as Jo cycled to the sweet-shop, he had wished her good morning. And Jo had stopped and said yes, it was a great day, just right for sailing, and Ted had said, 'D'you know, that's just what I was thinking.'

So Ted fiddled in the garage for a while and then the Rev came over with Jaz and Alex, and even Maggie Thomas came out to look, and together they pulled the dinghy on the trailer down to the slipway and cheered at the splash as it went into the water.

The Rev was elected to have the first trip with Ted. They sailed downriver to the harbour mouth, the outboard 'put-putt'-ing gently and leaving a shallow foam-edged furrow in its wake.

Jo, Gary, Jaz and Alex raced round the path to meet them at the harbour mouth. When they got there Ted and Pastor Walcott were hoisting the sails and getting ready to sail out to sea. Ted was shouting instructions about sheets and shrouds and centreboards, and the Rev was frowning and scratching his bald patch and trying to look as if he knew what he was doing. They hadn't even loosed the moorings when the boom swung across and nearly knocked him overboard, and everyone roared with laughter, even Ted, who lost his footing and ended up sitting in a puddle in the bottom of the boat.

And then Gary started trying to jump off the jetty and climb aboard, so as a distraction Jo and Jaz took him off for a tour round the old army pillboxes. When they looked up again, *Mary Jane*'s sails were full and she was skimming across the glimmering water like a dream.

The concrete pillboxes, built half a century ago against the Germans, were sunk in grassy mounds round the old coastguard station. It was a great place, Alex decided, for playing army. He raced around—repelling a vast enemy invasion—with Gary chasing after him and imitating his 'Ack-ack-ack-ack'. Jo and Jaz watched them and laughed until their sides ached.

And then there was a 'Hello' from the jetty and Ted and the Rev were back, and it was someone else's turn to don lifejacket and play crew member. In between sea-going excursions, they played Hide and Seek and Kick the Can, and ate sandwiches and chocolate biscuits as the day passed by. They hardly noticed the shadows lengthening and the distant church clock chiming the hours. It wasn't until the breeze on their sun-burnt skins suddenly made them shiver that the Rev looked at his watch and groaned. 'It's Hove Fellowship Harvest Supper. We're supposed to be there in half an hour.'

Throughout the day, Gary had formed an attachment to Alex. Now it was time to leave he clung on and tried to go with him.

'Well, why not?' asked Jaz. 'They said bring a friend. He might liven the place up a bit.'

'A bit too much,' protested Ted, but the Rev insisted. 'He'll be fine. They're good folks, they won't mind. Give yourself a break. Good, that's settled. The question is, however are we going to make it in time?'

But that was easy. *Mary Jane* became a ferry and the Walcotts were dropped barefoot and salty across the river by the yacht club. Jo leaned back on the mound by the coastguard station and gave a last wave as they disappeared into the town. She cast her eye along the river. No, it wasn't a bad old place to live, not at times like these.

A group of canoeists were paddling upriver, like a family of ducks, v-shaped ripples spreading behind them. Idly her eye followed their path. It led her to *Peggy Sue*, still moored next to the scrap-yard, abandoned for good, it seemed, in her grey unfinished camouflage. Suddenly Jo leant forward, eyes tightened in concentration. She was still staring when Ted returned, cap askew and nose and cheeks glowing pink.

He followed her gaze. 'What's so interesting about the rubbish tip?'

'No, that boat. It belonged to Sebastian. You know, the smuggler. I could have sworn I saw something moving on board.'

He stared with her, but whatever it had been—a seagull perhaps, rubbish blowing in the breeze—it was no more.

'Well, young lady, it's time for supper. Your mum's offered me some pizza tonight.'

'Has she indeed?' thought Jo, but Ted just grinned at her raised eyebrows.

'Friends, that's all. Friends in adversity. I've been a long time without any—my own making, I know.'

He smiled at Jo as he climbed down into the little dinghy and tossed her a lifejacket.

'Thanks for the help. I've laid a few ghosts today.'

He began untying the ropes. 'Come on, let's head for home.'

They made a wide arc through the sea and came back into the river mouth. Jo stretched her legs, licked her salty lips and trailed her hand in the water. The river was quiet now, all the pleasure craft in for the evening; the fishermen not due out till the next tide. Only one other boat disturbed the peace as they tacked upstream. It was a small boat, heading downriver at a speed that rocked *Mary Jane* in its wake. 'Idiot,' muttered Ted, and Jo ducked her head below the sail to look. It was a familiar boat—very familiar, Jo had even been on it—and it contained a familiar bronzed, blond figure. Sebastian, standing at the helm like some reckless Greek god, was racing out to sea.

'Turn round, quick, come on.' Jo was so frantic that Ted obeyed her automatically. He looked more closely at the figure on the little motor boat and then he understood.

The wind caught them on the turn and they skimmed out again between the harbour walls, but even so, the distance between them and Sebastian was widening by the second.

'We'll never keep up.'

'Try, just try. Don't lose him,' Jo pleaded. She didn't really know why. She just knew that people like him ought to be stopped. People like him, who got rich and sleek while people like her sister got exploited and destroyed, ought to be punched on the nose and knocked overboard and held under until they screamed for mercy.

'We'd be more sensible to turn round and alert the police. They could catch him when he comes back.'

'How'd we know he's coming back? We can't lose him

now. Let's at least find out which way he's heading.'

But Ted didn't really need persuading. He understood what it was to be angry with those whose
recklessness left others crushed.

Together they willed the boat to move faster, and
stared helplessly as Sebastian disappeared out to sea. In
a matter of minutes he would be nothing more than a
dot on the horizon.

Ted delved into a hatch and handed Jo a pair of
binoculars.

Jo, focusing just in time, saw the dot grow once
more into a boat which, as she looked, turned east.
'He's running parallel with the coast, towards Brighton.
He seems to have slowed.'

'Good, we're in with a chance then. Keep him in
sight and we'll stay in closer to the shore.'

Several times Jo thought they'd lost him. The waves
were whipping up now, and the sun had long since
dipped behind the Downs. Grey clouds crowded in.
She shivered, grateful for the warmth of the lifejacket
over her T-shirt.

'D'you think he knows we're following?' asked Ted.

'Dunno. He seems to have looked back a few times,
but I can't really tell.'

'Here.' Ted handed Jo his yachting cap. 'Tuck your
hair in that. Just in case he's got binoculars too.'

On and on they went, skimming the waves, vaguely
aware of the passing kaleidoscope on their left: street
lamps, service stations, hotels. And all the while their
eyes were fixed out on the horizon and a dim black dot
disappearing in a slate-grey sea.

'I've lost him,' admitted Jo at last. 'But please let's
carry on. If he turns in to land we might catch up.'

Ted sighed and said it was ridiculous, but he did admit that the wind was about as favourable as it could be. They kept on and on until they passed the two piers, one a dark abandoned hulk, the other bright and so close they could hear the ping of arcade games and screams from the Waltzer. Still Jo scanned the horizon hopefully.

'There!' she said triumphantly. 'That's him. Look, there. He's coming right in. P'rhaps he's going into the Marina.'

Ahead of them was the giant concrete lego that marked out the yacht haven.

'Yes, he's going in. Oh, no, he's not.'

Sebastian obviously had a further destination, under or beyond the shadowy chalk cliffs.

'OK, that's it,' said Ted, turning the boat.

'We can't give up now,' pleaded Jo. 'If we're daft enough to come this far . . .'

'You know,' Ted mused, 'when we launched *Mary Jane* this morning, I thought it'd just be a short spin. We're not prepared for a round-the-world yacht race.'

The disappointment on Jo's face could not be hidden. He sighed. 'All right, just a bit further. But under outboard. It'll be steadier and far less obvious.'

Gleefully Jo helped lower the sails. 'But won't he hear us?'

'Above his engine noise? I shouldn't think so.'

And so they glided on past the Marina entrance. The cliffs loomed above them now, with a windmill outlined against the sky and ever fewer lights to guide them.

'It's not called Black Rock round here for nothing,' said Ted. Sure enough, dark, threatening shapes loomed close under the surface of the water. On they went until Jo began to feel they could be lost forever in the inky blackness. Of Sebastian there was no sight or sound.

Ted turned the boat around. 'Let's get back. Your mother will be wondering what's happened to us.'

'Wondering!' thought Jo. 'That's an understatement. She'll be going frantic.'

'We'll stop at the Marina. Contact the police or Customs or whoever, and give her a ring too.'

'Yeah, fine,' said Jo dully. 'Can we get some chips, I'm starvin'.'

She never knew what it was that made her turn and look behind her. But what she saw made her hiss, 'Hold on a minute,' and lunge for the binoculars. She spanned them across an expanse of nothing and then pointed. 'There, did you see it?'

'What?'

'A light. I'm sure it was ... Look!'

This time Ted saw it too, the flash of a torch, just off shore and much too near for comfort. Ted killed the engine. Only the gentle lapping of the waves broke the silence, until their ears adjusted and they caught the distant buzz of Sebastian's engine.

The torch flashed one more time. Then it was extinguished and they could do nothing but stare in frustration at the shifting shadowy sea. And then the moon came to their aid, gliding out from behind the clouds and showing Sebastian's silhouette clearly against the dimly reflecting waters.

'He's circling,' whispered Jo. 'There's something in the water. A buoy. He's tying up to it.'

The motor noise changed to an almost inaudible tick-over.

'It looks like he's hauling something up. Oh, no. He's drifted round. I can't see. P'raps he's lowering something. I dunno. Whatever's he up to? Oh, stink.'

An unexpectedly big wave swept *Mary Jane* inshore and a disturbing graunching noise told them they had hit rock. The binoculars jolted from Jo's hands, and she grabbed for the sides of the boat as *Mary Jane* tipped ominously. Ted grappled with an oar to push them off and Jo scrambled over to try and help.

'Get back,' he yelled urgently. 'Put your weight on the other side.'

But the waves were coming faster now, and so strongly that the spray broke over their heads. The harder he pushed, the more the sea drove them back.

Then came a sudden stillness, when they seemed to have broken free. Jo turned round once more to search for Sebastian, but the clouds chose that same moment to cover the moon and he disappeared, swallowed up in the darkness.

And then the waves were pounding again, and the black rocks loomed almost in front of their noses.

Ted and Jo clung on helplessly and in the distance the sound of a revving engine and the faintest glow of a white wake told them Sebastian was getting away.

Mary Jane creaked and cracked and swung round helplessly, until a devastating crunch told them the rocks had done their worst. A huge wave broke over them, filling the little boat with water and leaving Jo gasping for breath.

'Shipwreck,' she yelled. 'Shall we swim for it?'

Ted's answer was lost in the crashing of the waves.

20

Home from the Sea

Jo sat in the Marina Customs Office wearing a huge borrowed sweater that smelt comfortingly of sweat and pipe tobacco. She clasped a steaming mug of tea and the events of the last couple of hours seemed like a big confusing dream.

She remembered how the boat had rocked and her hands slipped as she grabbed for the rocks. Then somehow she was in the freezing inky torrent, with her mouth and nose filling with salt water that made her choke.

And then there had been the relief of discovering a ledge of rock where she could stand only waist-deep, followed by the shock of seeing *Mary Jane* suddenly breaking free and being swept out to sea, with Ted clinging on desperately. Somehow she had slithered and scrambled across the rocks, clutching blindly at limpet-encrusted outcrops, until at last she waded ashore and ran gasping and panting along the under-cliff path to the Marina.

She stumbled, vaguely aware of her grazed knees and elbows, towards the nearest pool of light, a moored cruiser. Men in navy blazers and women in silk shirts and pearls glanced at her dripping be-draggled figure and turned back to their sherry glasses. She found a small voice, most unlike her own, saying, 'Please, I need help.'

And now here she was sitting safe and warm in front of the glowing bars of an electric fire, while Ted, rescued by the coastguards, dried off and *Mary Jane*, battered but surviving, rocked gently against the harbour wall.

The coastguards had barely masked their disapproval of such foolhardy trippers, and Jo's explanation of smugglers had brought a response of, 'Young lady, this is no time to play games.'

But at last they'd listened and phoned Customs and Excise who agreed, yes, it could be suspicious, and to send them over. They were handed on to two jovial bearded characters who asked a lot of questions and seemed quite unsurprised that Sebastian should be visiting a buoy in the middle of nowhere.

'What these jokers do,' explained the tall grey-bearded officer, 'if they think things are getting too hot for them, is to put their stash of drugs, or gems, or whatever in a waterproof container and just throw it overboard. You'd be surprised what you can find on the sea bed. The trouble is there's an awful lot of sea out there and we can't search all of it. It could lie there for years, until they think the coast is clear—so to speak.'

'Only it wasn't,' said the short tubby one with the ginger beard. 'You turned up.'

'So will you arrest him now?'

'I'm afraid it's not that simple. Even if our boys can catch up with him—and he's got a good head start—we've got no hard evidence. He could be an innocent young man trying to catch lobsters for all we know. And if he is our man, we may want to leave him—see who he passes the stuff on to.'

They made some phone calls: alerting Customs in Shoreham and setting Maggie Thomas' fevered imagination at rest.

'Now you just sit tight, young lady,' said Ginger-Beard, 'while we take your dad out to look for this buoy.'

'He's not my dad,' protested Jo. 'And I'm coming too.'

But they looked at her chattering teeth and shivering arms and shook their heads. 'Enough adventures for one night, young lady.'

'Don't young lady me,' muttered Jo. 'I'm coming.'

But they were adamant. 'Anyway, young ... miss, chances of finding anything are pretty well nil. We'll give it a try, but even if we can find the spot, there's probably nothing there now.'

So Jo sat in the little office, before the glow of the fire until her eyelids drooped and her head nodded. In her dream she heard her mother's voice. She was very angry with someone Jo couldn't see. Words like 'Irresponsible' and 'Ridiculous risks' filtered through to her. 'Mum's going great guns,' thought Jo, 'must be some Greenpeace demo'. She could see her now at the front of a row of protesters. She was surprised when the policeman came down from his horse and started pleading with Mum. 'Maggie, I'm sorry. It really wasn't my idea,' he said in a voice which sounded very much like Ted's. 'Anyway, she's safe.'

And then she dreamed of sailing over dark seas, until a creak jolted her awake. Afraid of sinking, she opened her eyes to see Mum and Ted, and was surprised to find

Mum wasn't cross any more. Drowsily she was aware of being half-walked, half-carried to Mum's Mini and of stumbling into bed as the clock across the river struck midnight.

'Nothing! You mean after all that they didn't arrest him?'

Jo paced angrily through Ted's living-room with Gary hanging onto her arm.

'Couldn't find a thing. They've been back in daylight and swept the area pretty thoroughly, but if there was a buoy there, it's not there now.'

'But didn't they catch him? Surely if they'd searched him?'

'They lost him. By the time the Shoreham guys came out, he'd gone. They found the little motor launch tied up by his fishing boat. But he must have driven away. They think he might have been back on the houseboat, but there's been no sign of him here since I got back. They've searched all three boats, but there's nothing. They said they were grateful, but there's absolutely no evidence. All they've got is a report from some other young girl...'

'Jaz.'

'Exactly, but that proves nothing either. Without hard facts there's nothing else they can do.'

'You believe it, don't you?'

'Look Jo, I'll believe it's possible, but really there's nothing to go on. He could have just gone for a spin for the hell of it. It was only you that saw the buoy.'

'You don't believe me.'

'I believe you thought you saw it. But it was a long way away and very dark.'

'No one believes us. There's Abby gone missing and Dimitri dead, and he just sails away into the sunset. It's ... it's ... out of order, that's what!'

Her anger upset Gary. He let go of her arm and clattered up the stairs, hitting out wildly at the walls as he went. Jo tried to follow but Ted barred her way.

'No, you'll only upset him more. I can't afford that.'

Jo noticed the shadows under Ted's eyes and with a pang of guilt remembered his health. He'd been through all that last night, and it was all her idea.

'Sorry, sorry, I'll go.' Jo backed out and kicked her way disconsolately down the river path.

Mum was annoyed, Gary upset, Ted ill, and it was all her fault. Sebastian had got away free, and everyone thought the idea of him being a smuggler was stupid.

Almost without thinking, she headed for the one person who was on her side.

Jaz was sitting in the back row of the little chapel, pleasantly sleepy as the preacher's all-too-familiar voice rose and fell. Her wandering thoughts were disturbed by the creak of the chapel door and a shuffling as someone slipped in at the end of the row. Jo! In a church. Miracles did happen!

But Jo's attention was far from holy things. Bending forward so she could see Jaz, she mouthed, 'Sebastian'.

Jaz raised her eyebrows in reply.

'I've seen him,' said Jo, in a loud whisper.

Pastor Walcott stopped and peered over his half-glasses in the direction of the disturbance. Several other pairs of eyes turned to look, notably Mrs Walcott, who fixed Jaz with the sort of look that was not to be ignored.

'Later,' whispered Jaz and fixed her gaze innocently on the pulpit.

Jo sighed. She was squashed against the end of the pew, but moving looked like creating more aggro. And that I don't need, she thought.

So she stayed put and listened vaguely while the Rev told some story about a bloke who got chucked in prison for something he didn't do. 'Misunderstood, rejected and alone,' declaimed the Rev in dramatic mode.

'Know how you felt, mate,' thought Jo, and watched a drowsy bluebottle bashing against the window-panes. She knew this story. It was the amazing technicolor dreamcoat fella, they'd done it at Mill Park Juniors. Well, things turned out all right for him.

She willed the bluebottle to find its way to the only broken pane, and was absurdly pleased when it did. She began to count the number of cracked panes in the old high chapel windows. She stopped at twenty-seven, her attention drawn by what the Rev was saying.

'Have I ever told you,' he began, 'how God spoke to me in a lavatory?'

A rustle indicated that the remark had had the desired effect of waking his audience up.

'When I was eleven,' he continued, 'back in Guyana, I got a scholarship to a boarding school. All us "free" boys were given jobs to do. Mine was cleaning the toilets. I was lonely and frightened and angry with being treated like the lowest of the low. So I thought, I'll show 'em. They'll have the cleanest, shiniest floors there's ever been. But some of the other boys had been sent out to do the gardens. I'd got those floors just sparkling, when someone came in with muddy feet and tramped right across. I felt very righteous and patient, and I went over it all again. The next time it happened, I wasn't quite so patient. The fourth time, I was hopping mad. The fifth person who came in, I shouted at. It was the headmaster. He just turned and walked out and I felt like crying. I went and locked myself in a cubicle. It was then God spoke to me.

'Now I'll admit I'm a bit suspicious of people who are always talking as if they hear God speaking in a real live voice. But this was ... so real I bent and looked under the door to see if someone else had come in. But the floor was clear. No more feet.

'The voice said, "I saw you do the job the first time." That's all. But I understood it. God knew I'd tried hard. Even if everyone else thought I'd made a lousy job of it, he saw the truth. They looked on the outside, God looked on the heart.

'It taught me something else, that voice. It showed me that God understood every little thing that was going on inside me, and even when I blew it, he never gave up. And all these years since, I've discovered it's the same. That's why I get so excited about him. Hallelujah!'

The Rev's shiny face was split by a huge infectious grin. Jo couldn't help grinning back, because what that little story had told her was that God understood her too.

And Jaz understood. Jaz believed her, and Jaz in typical fashion was convinced it would all work out.

'Coincidences like that don't just happen. They're bound to get him soon. And you can't say I'm the one who always has adventures any more.'

She had a practical suggestion too. 'Let's offer to take Gary out this afternoon. Give Ted a rest.'

Ted was grateful but he didn't want a rest. 'No, I'll admit I'm tired, but I'm beginning to enjoy a bit of excitement. Tell you what. Your mum offered to take me back to the Marina to inspect *Mary Jane*'s damage. Could you look after Gary here while I go?'

After Ted and Maggie had driven off, Gary was in restless mood. First Jo made biscuits with him. Gary enjoyed cutting out the shapes and eating all the leftover bits, but it didn't take that long, so Jaz cleared up the mess while Jo got out paper, scissors and glue. Jaz and Jo got carried away with a big collage of bright paper shapes, but Gary got bored and wandered up to his bedroom.

Jaz cleared up the bits of paper, while Jo went upstairs. As usual, Gary was staring out over the river, endlessly twisting a piece of rope around between his fingers.

'Oh, Gary, don't you ever get bored with that?' asked Jo exasperated.

Gary turned to her with an unexpected smile. 'Shiny,' he said, pointing.

'What? Oh, good. Shiny. Well, I suppose it keeps you happy.'

She sat on the bed and made a monster from Lego. Jaz came up and started folding Gary's scattered clothes.

'You'll make someone a wonderful wife,' said Jo.

'No fear, I wouldn't go picking up clothes after some fella,' retorted Jaz.

'Gary's a fella.'

'That's different.'

It *was* different, they each thought sadly, watching Gary. They thought of the might-have-beens: Gary crewing his dad's boat, sitting his A-levels; of the books he'd never read, the friends he'd never have.

He can't do much, thought Jo, but I still like him. He's quite lovable really. Most people were lovable, she supposed, once you got to know what was hidden underneath. Gary was lovable because there was nothing hidden. You couldn't tell how much he understood, but his feelings were all there on the surface.

Right now he was excited about something, jabbing the window pane with his fingers. 'Shiny,' he repeated. 'Shiny.'

'What's he on about?' wondered Jaz, and went to look. There were always tin cans on the path, and Greg in the end houseboat reconditioned old motorbikes, so there was always lots of scrap metal there. But it was not there that Gary was looking. He was pointing straight out of the window towards Sebastian's empty houseboat. Just to one side of it, half-buried in mud and about two metres beyond the boat's little jetty, was a large metal container. It was a sort of metal beer keg, but to Gary it looked like a giant tin can and he wanted to get it.

'Yeah, Gary, shiny,' she agreed. 'But you can't have that one.'

It didn't strike her as unusual. The river bed was littered with scrap: wooden spars, milk crates, old tyres. At low tide you saw all the junk that was hidden the rest of the time.

Jo looked up enquiringly from her Lego.

'Just some old metal container in the mud,' explained Jaz, and went back to sorting socks.

'Shiny,' insisted Gary, getting agitated now that no one was taking notice. Now he'd seen it, it had become a desired object, a rich treasure just out of reach. 'New shiny,' he repeated.

'New shiny?' Jo looked up sharply at this unexpected extra vocabulary.

She came to the window. 'Where, Gary, where?'

He pointed.

'It's a new one, is it?' she asked.

Gary agreed. 'New shiny.'

'You mean it wasn't there before?'

Gary nodded.

She stared at the container, buried deep in the mud where only the lowest of tides would expose it. It was well hidden. In fact, you wouldn't be able to see it from the path, or from across the river. The high vantage point of Gary's window was practically the only place it was visible.

Excited, Jo summoned Jaz back to the window and explained her theory.

Jaz grinned at Gary. Gary grinned back, sensing that for once someone else was as interested in his discovery as he was.

'Gary,' she said, 'I think you've just done something really useful.'

21

Mud, Glorious Mud

'OK then, Gary, me old mate. How about we go and get that shiny?' asked Jo.

Gary just grinned.

'You're not going to let him go in the mud?' asked Jaz, suddenly prim.

'Yeah, why not? It's in a good cause. Give him a bit of fun. Take yer shoes off, Gary.' Jo's feet were already bare and she was rolling up her jeans.

'You're sure Sebastian isn't in there?'

'There's no sign of life, see for yourself. Anyway, his Range Rover's not in the car park.'

Jaz looked anxiously. The curtains were open and you could see clearly into the tiny cabin.

A distant rumble turned her eyes to the sky. The glorious weather was breaking and the clouds were low and heavy. A dark streaking in the sky over the Downs made her realize that it was already raining in the west.

She glanced down. The tide, she noticed, was coming up fast.

'Come on then.' Jo had a gleam in her eye like some manic commando on a death or glory mission. 'Let's go.'

Enthusiastically, she and Gary tiptoed into the mud. Immediately they sank up to their ankles with satisfying squelching noises. Gary toppled and put down his hands to steady himself. He now had sludge grey gloves and sludge grey ankle socks. A fly darted across his face and he rubbed at the itch.

Jaz, watching from the bank, shrieked with laughter. Jo turned to look and Gary, trying to catch up, charged into her. For a moment they wobbled precariously, but somehow they made it to the shiny. The tide was trickling nearer in tiny rivulets, noticed Jaz, and the depressions left by their footsteps were filling with water.

Gary tugged at the canister. It was bigger and buried deeper than they had realized. Jo tried to help but it seemed stuck fast. They were both digging, scrabbling in the grey ooze like frantic puppy dogs, when the first drops of rain came.

Jaz, on the bank, saw the lightning sheet across the town. Gary only heard the massive thunder clap, and jumped up in panic, knocking Jo backwards. Dripping with mud, Jo ran frustrated fingers through her hair. Delighted, Gary copied her. They gave the the canister one last tug. It came away with a squelch, and sent them both sprawling. But it was not quite free. Fixed to its side was a heavy chain still leading into the mud. Slowly but surely, Jo followed its path, lifting it from the sludge until she reached the end.

'Oh no,' she muttered in frustration, and then, 'Oh yes!'

The chain was looped around Sebastian's jetty, padlocked in place. She did a little war dance of glee, which left her covered in dirty splatters.

Her reaction left Jaz baffled. 'What's so good about that? It just means you can't take it.'

'What's so good,' explained Jo, drawing dark swirls on her upper arms, 'is that it proves someone put it here. Someone who didn't want it moved. Someone who knew that what was inside was so valuable it had to be padlocked and buried in mud.

'Listen, go into Ted's garage. I think he's got some tools there. See if you can find something that'll saw metal.'

'But what if Sebastian comes back?'

'What if we get struck by lightning or swept out by the tide? Get a move on, that's what!'

Gary was frustrated with his shiny. It was too heavy and he couldn't carry it away. But he was enjoying the mud. Cheerfully he sat down and plastered every bit of himself until only two white-rimmed eyes peered out at them.

'Yeah Gary, you're a cool dude,' said Jo. 'Yessir, you an' me both.' She lifted Gary's hand and slapped it in salute. Gary liked the hand-slapping idea and repeated it vigorously.

Jaz returned with a saw. 'Is this right?'

'Dunno, let's try.'

Urgently Jo sawed at the metal. The tide was beginning to swirl round her knees. 'It works, but it's gonna take for ever.'

Jaz dashed back to the garage. She returned barefoot and with a length of wire in her hands.

'Keep sawing, but I've got another idea. I'm coming down.'

And then Jaz was in the muddy water, and fiddling with her bent wire in the keyhole of the padlock.

'Didn't know you could pick locks.'

'I can't, but there's always a first time.'

The rain began to fall in earnest now, and Gary, bored with the game, abandoned his shiny and waded back to the bank.

'Gary, come back.' Jo lunged after him and missed. Gary headed straight for the house.

'Oh no,' Jaz groaned, picturing the muddy footprints across the carpet.

'Don't stop now,' hissed Jo. 'The tide's nearly beating us.'

It was indeed eddying around their thighs now. Jaz crouched down, picking the padlock unseen underwater.

'Gotcha,' she yelled triumphant and leapt up. The water was up to her waist.

She held the open padlock aloft, and together they carried their prize out of the river and back to the safety of the house.

The desk sergeant at Shoreham Police Station was having a boring day. Now the weather had turned there were no day-trippers asking silly questions, there were no parking offences on Sundays, and even the burglars seemed to be taking a day of rest. He tuned his radio to the cricket but rain had stopped play. He stirred his mug of tea and wished he was at home tending his dahlias.

A commotion outside made him lower his feet from the desk and button his collar, but he stopped midbutton-hole at the sight that met his eyes.

Three wet and grimy figures stood there, like refugees from a particularly nasty gunge tank. Rain still trickled in muddy rivulets down their faces, mud clung to their ears, necks, arms. A pungent river smell came in with them.

They were young, these figures, only teenagers. The biggest girl was clutching something like a beer keg.

'Here's your evidence,' she announced, dumping it on the counter. 'Now will you believe me?'

In an untidy inner office, four police officers and two Customs men stood in reverent amazement around the metal canister.

Its contents, a heap of packets wrapped in black plastic, were tipped on a desk in a hastily cleared space.

'Street value? Around one and a half million, I'd say,' said the tall black-moustached Customs officer.

'Biggest haul in our waters,' said the tubby, bearded Customs man with glee.

'Ah, but it was up-river,' said a policeman in uniform.

'Still the responsibility of Customs.'

'But it did come to us first,' put in the desk sergeant. 'If your boys hadn't made that ham-fisted raid all those months ago . . .'

A polite but cold discussion ensued. It seemed to have something to do with who should take the credit.

'Oi, we found it,' Jo reminded them.

'Yes indeed,' said the tall Customs man, who seemed to have taken the position of authority. 'And we're indebted to you. This is a great step forward in crime prevention.'

The two Customs officers fell to discussing where the drugs might have come from. In her head, Jaz nicknamed them Captain Hook and Captain Haddock. Jo tried to stop Gary dismantling vital police records.

'Excuse me,' ventured Jaz after a while, 'but what about Sebastian?'

'Yeah,' agreed Jo. 'After all this he's still got away.'

'He has for now,' agreed Captain Haddock, 'but he'll be back. You don't leave one and a half million lying in the mud and forget about it. He'll be back, sure as anything, and then we'll be waiting for him.'

'But if he comes back now, it won't be in the mud.'

'Oh yes it will,' explained Captain Hook. 'Because we're going to put it back.'

'Put it back!' exploded Jo. 'All those disgusting drugs.'

'Well, not quite,' he acknowledged. 'We've got to get busy. It's what we call "dummying-up". What your Sebastian gets when he hauls it up again will be about five kilos of harmless powder, with a little bit of heroin left in to fool him. We'll set the trap and just sit back and wait for him to creep right into it.'

At the next low tide, around two in the morning, there was lots of strange, secret activity on the river bank. Ted, watching from the upper window, chuckled while Gary snored contentedly behind him.

He could just make out the shadowy figures trying to squelch quietly, and Jo and Jaz, who had been given special permission to stay up, trying to point out just exactly where they'd found the canister.

Still chuckling, Ted went down to put the kettle on. He was officially in on the secret, because the Customs officers had asked permission to use his house as a look-out point. They'd brought in their equipment: radio, video—and two officers who were installed at the window of the tiny box-room next to Gary's. They'd be there round the clock now, for however long it took. He was going to be seeing a lot of these lads, thought Ted, so he might as well make them feel at home right away.

Jaz tiptoed muddily through the kitchen door. 'Four cocoas and three teas, please.'

When Pastor Walcott came to collect Jaz and escort Jo down the path, Ted and the Customs men were seated round the kitchen table and joking like old friends.

'I've a feeling all this could be the best thing to happen to Ted in a long while,' said the Rev as they bid Jo goodnight. 'You did well, girls.'

'And Gary,' reminded Jo. 'He's the one who spotted it. He did well too.'

It was four o'clock and the sky was lightening before Jo finally drifted to sleep.

'Wow, God,' she addressed the pink-streaked sky, 'they did believe me. It did come right.'

Her eyes closed and her thoughts drifted in confusion. She pictured Ted as they'd left him, head thrown back and roaring with laughter. She pictured Sebastian in a similar pose, with blond hair flying against a blue sky. Funny, in her head she knew he was evil, but in her heart she still found it hard to believe.

She sighed. Back to normal—school tomorrow. The Customs men had told her firmly to stay out of the way, and not a word to a soul. She smiled ruefully to herself. This was the best excuse she'd ever had for being late, and she wouldn't be able to tell anyone!

It was all down to them now. The adventure was over, she thought as the sun slipped up beyond the footbridge and she slipped down into oblivion.

But in that she was quite wrong.

22

No News and Good News

Jaz awoke with a start. It was 9.15.

'Oh no, mega-late. Why hasn't Mum yelled at me yet?'

Then she remembered. Mum had said that after all the excitement and the late night, she'd write a note excusing her from school 'for personal reasons'.

A lie-in on Monday morning. What a luxury. She turned over and snuggled down. Then she became aware of what had woken her so suddenly—the doorbell ringing insistently.

'Why doesn't someone answer it?' Jaz buried her head under the pillow.

This was some persistent caller and it dawned on her that Mum had just popped out to take Alex to school. She stumbled downstairs and peered through the cobbled glass with bleary eyes. She made out two faces she recognized, the Customs officers from the Investigation Unit. She drew her dressing-gown more tightly round her and opened the door.

'No, no. Really, I don't think I could.' Jaz looked at Mum for support.

'Well, of course, we wouldn't force you to do anything you don't want to do,' said the woman officer. 'And it's up to your parents as well. It's just that it might help us considerably.'

'And our boys would be right behind you. You wouldn't be at any kind of risk.'

'But why Jasmine?' asked Mum, looking worried.

They explained it again. The suspect had come back very early this morning, just hours after they'd replaced the canister with its fake contents. 'He's retrieved the drugs but he's very edgy. We think he'll try and find someone else to deliver the goods. And that's when we wondered if . . .'

Jaz hunched up in the armchair, thinking desperately. Mum looked equally worried.

'Of course, he may not be willing to trust you again,' said the woman officer. 'It's a long shot, but if you were willing, it might be worth trying.'

'It's not that you have to actually deliver the goods. All we want from you is to collect them and start on the journey,' explained the man.

'But how does your decoy take over?' asked Mum.

'It's easy. Jasmine goes into the Ladies at Victoria Station or wherever, and comes out a different woman. One of our officers—same colouring, same build, same clothes, but if anyone is watching, it'll fool them.'

'Why should someone be watching?'

'You'd be amazed. There's plenty of other rogues would like to get their hands on that sort of loot. Smith's dead shifty. We're not sure if it's us he's afraid of, or a rival gang.'

'Smith?' queried Jaz.

'Not half so glamorous as Sebastian Raphael, is it?

But that's his real name—Ray Smith. But forget we told you, and under no circumstances tell anyone else. As far as you're concerned he's still Sebastian.'

'But if someone's following me, they could attack me before I turned into a Customs officer.'

'That's why our boys will be right there. Believe me, it'd be more than our lives are worth to put you into real danger.'

With relief, Jaz heard the key turn in the lock. Dad was here, he'd say no.

'Well,' said Dad after it had all been explained again, and he and Mum had had a hurried consultation, 'if you can really assure us that it's quite safe. And if it really will help catch these terrible people ... Well then, it's up to Jasmine.'

Thanks, Dad!

'OK,' Jaz heard herself saying, 'if it'll help.'

The first bit was the worst, she told herself, as she hovered on the path.

The phone had rung at 2.30. 'Now,' they'd told her. 'He's gone jogging. Get ready and you can just happen to be there on the path when he comes back.'

Their timing was just perfect. She was about a hundred metres from *Shangri-La* when he came into view, jogging steadily. He broke into a sprint, his usual final test of stamina. Their paths crossed just before he got to his gate.

'Hello,' Jaz said timidly.

'Hi.' He hardly glanced at her, wiping the sweat from his brow as he passed.

'Sebastian!' She drew a determined breath and followed.

He looked up this time, slowing to a halt. 'Oh hi, it's you.' He hardly looked pleased to see her, but she persevered: 'Haven't seen you in ages. Thought you'd gone away.'

'Yes, I had.' He bent over with hands on knees, panting after his exertions. Jaz couldn't see his face.

'I wanted to see you,' Jaz continued, 'to say sorry—about the other week and not collecting your stuff and that. It was so stupid. The thing is, I'm not used to London, and I'm really ever so shy, and I got in a bit of a panic.'

She stopped, gulping for breath. Her heart was thumping as if she, and not he, had just run five miles.

Slowly he raised his head. His face was tense. Was it from suspicion, or anger, or even, it occurred to her, fear? For a moment he didn't speak, and his blue eyes searched her face.

'You see,' she continued, 'what I wondered was . . . I don't expect you to forgive me or anything, but if you could give me a second chance . . . I'm really cross with myself that I didn't talk to Max, and I'd like to try again. I do really want to be a dancer . . .'

His face relaxed, and a shadow of that wonderful smile crossed it. 'I don't think so. Max is far too busy right now. And you're too young. I like to do favours where I can, but really, you're only a kid. I shouldn't have got you into it.'

'I'm thirteen.' Jaz drew herself up to her fullest height.

'Sorry, there's no second chances in this business, I'm afraid.'

'Oh well, OK. But I'd still like to make it up to you. If there's ever anything I can do for you . . . like running errands.'

'Thanks, but business like mine is really too important. I've just got to have someone trustworthy.' He turned and shut the gate behind him. 'Go back to school and don't get mixed up in ... Come to think of it, shouldn't you be at school?'

'Oh, er, yes, er, no. I was off sick, but I'm feeling better. See you, then.'

Jaz watched him stride into *Shangri-La.* 'Oh well, I tried,' she thought with relief. 'Thank goodness that's over.'

But it wouldn't really all be over, Jaz and Jo agreed, until Sebastian was put behind bars.

They were in the gym storeroom, amid hoops and mats, while Jaz got on with her allotted task—sorting a great heap of coloured bands. It was worth it for the sake of somewhere quiet to talk, and what Jo and Jaz wanted most to talk about, and what must not be overheard, was Sebastian and the progress of the Customs' vigil.

For days Jo had cycled along the path, pretending not to look for the watchers in Ted's box-room or the 'twitchers' across the river. In fact, she rarely saw them, although she was sure they were still there. And she pretended not to look for Sebastian, but she knew he was still there too. The shiny, however, had gone. Something must be happening, but it was not all over.

Every morning, passing the newsagent's, Jaz looked for headlines like 'Drugs baron caught', or 'South coast smugglers intercepted'. She wrote her own sub-headings: 'Schoolgirl heroines alert police', 'Terror journey of courageous young dancer'.

When Miss Reeves saw them all over her rough book, Jaz said she was thinking of writing a story, and Miss Reeves was quite chuffed at these signs that her English teaching was not in vain.

But for now the story could not be told. The days passed by and Sebastian went for a jog twice a day, and finished painting *Peggy Sue*, and Jaz and Jo went to school.

Yes, this term Jo went to school—every day. She was even beginning to work. Something in Jo's life was changing. And part of the change could be summed up in the three envelopes she fished from her pocket, as she sat on the scuffed leather horse and watched Jaz sort bands.

The first contained a letter postmarked Birmingham.

Dear Jo,

I thought it was time I let you and Mum know where I was. Please don't say I told you so, but I'm at a rehab centre where they help you come off drugs. Yes, in the end I decided that I wasn't going to make it on my own.

This place isn't too wonderful—a bit like being back at school. And the withdrawal was ghastly—I don't ever, ever want to go through that again. But I've been clean for two weeks now. Early days, I know, but I'm beginning to think life might be worth living without those extortionate little packets.

I've been looking out for jobs, and there's a clothing manufacturer near here might take me on. It's starting at the bottom all right, but if I want to learn the trade I've got to be prepared for that. I might try for a post-graduate course in a couple of years. Not at Brighton though, I really need a new start.

So, little sis, THANKS. Honest, I mean it. Sorry for all the lousy things I said to you, and the even lousier things I thought about you! I didn't like it too much at the time, but I suppose I'm glad you never gave up.

Tell Mum I'll write. I'll come home sometime, but not yet. Don't rush me, the time's got to be right. Visitors are welcome here though, so why don't you come?

Go for it, kid. You're the tough one in this family.
Tons of love,
Abby

The second contained a note in dashing purple ink on a torn-off scrap of manuscript paper.

Dear Jo,
Thank you and well done.

Thank you for seeing how things really were with Abby when your Mum and I were too blind to notice.

Well done for chasing the drugs smuggler. Mum told me all about it. I'm amazed. Somehow my little baby has turned into a determined young woman before my very eyes.

I've missed so much of your growing-up. It saddens me far more than you can imagine. I know I've made a mess of things. I hope I'll get it right next time. Yes, Alison and I are to be married. She'd love

219

to meet you. Why don't you come up and stay one
weekend?

Love to my very special daughter,
Dad

The letter had a postscript in another, neater hand.

P.S. Your dad's not much good at remembering to
organize things, is he, so I hope you don't mind if I
do? Why don't you come next weekend? He's told me
so much about you, I hope we can be friends. I'll
make sure he phones.
Love, Alison

The first letter, when she had opened it, brought
tears of relief. Her reaction to the second was far more
complicated. 'I do feel pleased, but angry too. I can't
explain.'

'Try,' said Jaz.

'When you're a little kid, your mum and dad—and
even your big sister—are a bit like ... well, like God.
You know they're not perfect really, but they're so
much bigger than you. You think they must've got it
together. It's a bit of a shock when you discover
they've messed things up. At first it feels like they've
cheated you. I s'pose it's part of growing up.'

'Are you going to visit?'

'Abby, yeah. Mum an' me are going at half-term.
Dad, um ... I guess so. I don't know how I feel about
seeing him with someone new, but Alison seems OK. I
s'pose he deserves a second chance as much as anyone
else. He's only human after all.'

The third envelope contained a postcard. It had

pictures of New Forest ponies on the front, and on the back it read (in neat tidy writing) 'We are here. I rode a horse' and (in a meandering spidery scrawl) 'Gary'.

This was the other great change in the last few weeks. Gary had gone away to school. It was mostly thanks to Pastor Walcott, who was not above exploiting his position if it would help someone else. He'd made a nuisance of himself with Social Services until they'd found a residential school place and agreed to pay.

'And Gary loves it there, Ted says.'

'But I thought you said he hated it?' queried Jaz.

'He did at first. It was awful. He banged his head and yelled and kicked and clung to Ted. Mum and me had to drag him away—Ted, that is. And he got really stressed out. But he phoned at the weekend and Gary was fine. They said the art room had run out of shiny paper.

'It's a fabulous place. They've got dogs and cats and goats and rabbits, and woods all round, and an adventure playground, and they do pottery and there's tons of cartoon videos.'

'Doesn't Ted miss him, though?'

'Course. He was a right old grouch at first. But he keeps coming round to our place. Mum says she just feels sorry for him, but I'm not so sure. And he's started going through the newspaper and looking for jobs, and yesterday he went out and got this boring grey suit to wear for an interview. He never mentions the Customs bods in the box-room, but he knows masses of new jokes and he's much more cheerful. I reckon he was really lonely.'

Jo tucked her three precious envelopes back in her pocket. Each had taught her something about herself.

The first two told her she was no longer in Abby's shadow, no longer second-best. She was strong. There were second chances for her too, and she could be anything she wanted to be.

And the postcard reminded her of something else she'd discovered. She knew what she wanted to be. She'd looked at that school: its activity rooms and especially its art room. And she knew. Most people wouldn't think it was very important—teaching someone like Gary to cook an egg or write his name—but she knew it was. And she knew she'd be good at it.

So that's why Jodi Thomas surprised everyone by working this term. She had started to believe in herself.

23

Seize the Day

The trouble with big dramatic moments is that they don't happen when you want them to. When the weather's glorious, and you've got a new pair of Levis, and you feel ready for anything, you end up hanging around the house getting bored. When it's drizzling and you've got a cold and all you want to do is sit in front of daytime TV and cuddle a hot water bottle, that's when the big things come along.

Jaz was off school in hot water bottle mode when the phone call came.

It was the lunch hour and Jo had slipped out of school to come sick visiting. The remains of lunch were all around them. It was the sort you make yourself when parents aren't around—cereal with ice cream and strawberry sauce, crisps, yoghurts and hot chocolate that left a thick sludge in the bottom of the mugs. Jaz was in one of those states where you want the food until it's actually in front of you, so Jo had had most of it.

Jo sang tunelessly along with the TV as she scraped the ice cream tub clean: 'Just a friendly wave each morning, helps to make a better daaaay.'

'You ought to be back at school.'

'It's games,' said Jo, with deep gloom. 'OK, OK, I'll go—I just want to see if he gets to kiss her.'

It was then that the phone rang, insistently disturbing the latest Ramsay Street intrigue.

'It'll be for Dad,' said Jaz, not moving.

'He's not here.'

'I know.'

'They don't.'

'Well, you tell them.'

Jo picked up the phone. 'Reverend Walcott's secretary. How may I help you?'

A man's voice, deep, warm, familiar. 'I don't suppose Jasmine's there by any chance?'

She passed the phone over. Jaz's face registered irritation, shocked recognition, the faintest hint of being flattered and then pure panic.

'No, I couldn't . . . No really, I know I said that but . . . I'm not feeling too good . . . Yes, I did mean it . . . It's just that . . . I'd have to ask my parents . . . Now? . . . Yes, I do but . . . Hang on a minute . . .'

She held her hand over the phone. 'It's Sebastian, he wants me to do an errand for him,' she whispered.

Jo's eyes widened. 'Well, go on then. Do it.'

Jaz opened her mouth to protest, then shut it again. She closed her eyes and screwed up her face like a tiny child trying to say a prayer. It was exactly what she was doing, and just who she felt like.

She opened her eyes. 'Sorry, Sebastian, I told you I got in a panic easily. Course I'll do it. Just give me a few minutes and I'll be on my way.'

With trembling hands, Jaz dialled the number she'd been given.

'Customs and Excise, can I help you? . . . That'd be Mr Jefferson, but I'm afraid he's at a conference today. Can I ask you to phone back? . . . Oh, I expect you mean Miss Langford. No, she's at lunch. Can I take a message? . . . I'll give you the duty desk . . . It's ringing for you.'

It rang, on and on.

'Why was Sebastian so desperate?'

'I don't know. But I'm not going on my own.'

'I'll come with you.'

'Thanks, but I'm not going to go without someone official around. I've learnt my lesson there.'

'Try again.'

Jaz tried. 'Sorry, caller, we're trying to connect you,' said the voice, then——nothing.

'Oh come on,' Jo took the phone from Jaz's hand and put it down. 'I know the answer—it's simple.'

The river was flecked with white foam wavelets and spotted with raindrops as two figures on a bike crossed the footbridge.

'I'll go into Ted's the back way,' explained Jo to Jaz. 'The Customs people there have got a radio, and they'll be watching. They'll get things happening. Don't worry. Hang on at Sebastian's as long as you can. I'll catch up with you back here, or wherever he sends you with the loot. It'll be OK, honest.'

Jaz clung on, and didn't bother to answer. Her head felt as if it was stuffed with cotton wool, and every bit of her ached. It was all a bad dream, and she'd wake up very soon.

She felt all too awake when a pair of blue eyes looked out at her and a strong arm ushered her courteously into the cabin.

'Jasmine, this is so good of you. You're a real pal.'
Sebastian was writing a note and slipping it into an
envelope. 'No impresarios today, I'm afraid, but I
won't forget I owe you a favour. Heard about the new
Lloyd-Webber? Well, the choreographer's an old
girlfriend of mine.'

Jaz tried to look impressed.

'... I happen to know they need juvenile dancers,
so who knows? And listen, this is so simple. Not the
big bad city this time. Just Brighton. You know the
Marina? Good.'

He stapled and taped the small padded envelope.
'This is all there is, and there's nothing to bring back.
You know the little square in the Marina, all trendy
shops and a fountain? Go and stand by the fountain, the
one with flying fish sculptures. Be there by 3p.m..
There'll be a guy comes up to you, he knows what you
look like, just give it to him—but only if he knows your
name. And that's it.

'Don't look so worried.' He put a gentle hand under
her chin. 'Although you're very pretty when you're so
serious.'

He opened a wallet stuffed with notes and drew out
two twenties. 'Here, take your fares out of this and
keep the rest. You're a real friend.'

'Should I take a cab?'

'No, no, however you'd normally go.'

'But what if I miss this person? Shouldn't I know who
I'm looking for?'

'Sorry, can't name names, very important player.
Trying to keep a low profile.'

'Ooh, is it someone famous?' Jaz was a picture of
innocent awe.

'Absolutely. That's why we try and keep his where-abouts hush-hush. And I'd appreciate it if you didn't mention my address either, should anyone ask.'

'It's the press after you again, I bet!'

Sebastian nodded with an air of modest acknow-ledgment, and went to look out of the cabin window. Jaz noticed a couple of workmen at the end of the path.

'Terrible weather,' Sebastian remarked casually, turning away from the window. 'D'you want a drink before you go?'

He kept her there for some time, turning out a stream of amusing showbiz stories, and rising occasionally to check the windows. Jaz got up too, not looking at the Carters' dormer window, but giving a thumbs-up in that direction while Sebas-tian's back was turned, just in case anyone thought she was in danger.

'It sounds very glamorous,' ventured Jaz when the conversation flagged. 'But it must be hard. All that travel, always on the move.'

Sebastian sipped his mineral water. 'Better than the alternative—stuck behind a desk, every day, year in, year out. Getting the 8.15 every morning.'

'But all this secrecy. Don't you get lonely?'

'Not really. I can find company when I need it. Imagine being stuck with the same boring people all the time. Can't imagine anything worse, can you?'

'S'pose not.'

'But you're right. It's a hard life. When I've made enough money I'll retire. In fact,' he smiled to himself, 'I'm thinking of it quite soon.'

He paced to the window again. 'The rain's eased off now.'

'It hasn't,' thought Jaz, 'but the workmen have gone. He's decided the coast is clear.'

He handed her the envelope. 'Why don't you tuck it inside your jacket? It won't get wet, then.'

'And it'll be less obvious,' thought Jaz.

'OK, then. I'm on my way.'

'She's on her way,' said Jo to the two Customs officers. She had been watching with them from Ted's box-room. Her remark was unnecessary. They were already rushing down the stairs and out of the back door. Jo followed.

'Oh no. You're staying here.'

'But I promised.'

'Sorry, it's risky enough with one of you.'

'She's my friend.'

'Then do what's best for her,' said Ted, coming out of the kitchen and standing between Jo and the back door. The two men slipped out.

'Don't worry, love. We'll look after her. The relief team's on its way to keep an eye on our smuggler. Hold the fort till then.'

Jo and Ted took their place at the box-room lookout post. It had taken on a new life since Jo saw it last. Two easy chairs and some impressive electronics were crammed in among Ted's piles of junk. A video camera at the window meant they could view Sebastian's movements without a face appearing at the window. Behind them the radio crackled a message.

'Operation Whiteflower, subject in view ...'

'That's them,' said Ted.

'Whiteflower?'

'That's their code. Jasmine—white flower, get it?'

'Oh, very subtle.'

'Listen, the next shift should be here any minute. I'll go downstairs to let them in. Call me if anything happens.'

Jo settled down to watch.

'Subject approaching bus stop,' said the voice on the radio. 'There's some doubtful characters around, but we're right behind her.'

'Thank goodness for that,' thought Jaz as two burly men in leather jackets stepped behind her in the bus queue. She didn't recognize them, but they had the solid dependable look of plain-clothes men.

'Do you go to the Marina?' she asked loudly as she got on the bus.

'No, darlin', change at Old Steine,' said the driver.

It was a bit worrying that the leather jackets didn't follow her to the top of the bus, but she supposed that was OK.

She glanced behind her nervously as the bus pulled out. A kind mumsy lady behind her gave her a smile. Two seats back a stubble-chinned guy in blue denim stared fixedly out of the window. Hadn't he been behind her on the footbridge? Had he been there to hear her mention the Marina? She felt the envelope under her coat and said another prayer for courage.

'Dear God, keep Jaz safe,' thought Jo, and then: 'Why does she get all the excitement?' It was boring peering at the little video screen in the cramped room at absolutely nothing happening.

Just then something did. Sebastian came out into his cabin. He was wearing a track suit.

'He's just got changed,' she called. 'Looks like he's going out.'

Ted came up to see. 'Oh, 2.30. He'll be going jogging. He does that every day.'

'What, in the rain?'

'Every day. Believe me, we know all there is to know about that guy. I could tell you what he has for breakfast, when he goes to bed.'

'Don't bother.'

'He goes out jogging every day. Twice most days. Talk about a health freak.'

'His own health maybe.'

'Too right.' There was a quiet tapping on the back door. Ted went downstairs. 'Call if he goes out.'

Jo peered at the video screen once more. Sebastian was pacing up and down, talking on the phone. He rammed the aerial down, paced some more, then pulled it up again. That call made, he seemed to relax. He lifted a briefcase onto the table and took something out. Jo jumped up to the window to get a better look. He took out some papers and a little maroony-red book, the size of a small notebook. He picked up his wallet and some keys. All these he put into a small black bag. He picked it up and stepped out of sight behind the door. Then he was coming out, casual, empty-handed and relaxed.

'He's off,' called Jo.

Brighton had its seedy end-of-season look. The bouncy castle was deflated and there were puddles in the crazy golf. A few late holiday-makers huddled in the rusting salt-bleached shelters. No windsurfers now— the iron-grey sea was uninviting. Jaz remembered other journeys—to Abby's party, to Mick's café—when chasing drugs smugglers had all been a bit of a game. How long ago that seemed. She sighed and wished her throat didn't ache so much.

She peered round again. The lady behind smiled again. Jaz avoided her eyes. She looked beyond her to where Denim-Jacket sat as impassively as before. Across the aisle a man in a grey raincoat was looking around shiftily. Hadn't he got on at Shoreham too? He met her gaze and turned away.

The fear in the pit of her stomach wouldn't let her forget that this trip was all too much in earnest—but still, she couldn't avoid a smile. For all she knew, every one of the other passengers could be a villain in disguise!

What if she just made a run for it and took the parcel to the police? It must have some evidence in it. Surreptitiously she put a hand inside her jacket and felt the envelope. It didn't seem to have much in it. She felt something hard—a key perhaps?

If she got off now, Blue-Denim and Grey-Mac would see, but the Leather-Jackets, expecting her to go to the Marina, might not. She sat tight, and before long the bus was swinging inland, threading round the one-way system and past the onion domes of the Regency Pavilion.

'All change,' said the driver and, with as much calm and indifference as she could muster, Jaz got off and crossed the traffic to find a bus for the Marina.

As she waited at the crossing she glanced back. Yes, they were all following—Leather-Jackets, Grey-Mac and Blue-Denim. She found the right bus stop on the promenade. Waiting was awful. She stared blindly at the sea-front. It looked as dreary and miserable as she felt. She was relieved when a bus came almost immediately. Jaz took a seat near the door and watched Grey-Mac and Denim-Jacket pay their fares and pass without a glance to seats at the back. The bus driver was just churning out the last ticket when Jaz turned and noticed the Leather-Jackets. They were standing on the pavement, hailing a cab.

Jo watched Sebastian jog away down the river path. No different, relaxed and casual as always—and yet . . .

'Bum bag,' she said suddenly. 'That's it!'

Ted came up the stairs. 'That's another lot of officers arrived, and gone again. Following by car—routine precaution—do it every day . . . What's it?'

'Bum bag. He had a bum bag.'

Ted looked blank.

'On a belt, round his waist. It was hidden under his sweatshirt. A little bag—he put stuff in it.'

'Well, they'll be there to check he doesn't pick up his car . . . What sort of stuff?'

'Wallet, papers, a little book.'

'What kind of book?'

'A little red one. Sort of like . . . like . . .'

'A passport?'

'Oh dear God, like a passport!'

Ted and Jo stared at each other.

'Where does he usually go?'

'Along the path up-river, then when it's low tide he'll go up the road and back along the beach. At high tide he goes across the road, and carries on along the

232

path up-river. They can't follow there, so they watch him from the road. He usually runs to the end of the airfield, then back again.'

'Airfield! He's going to the airfield with a passport and the law's just sitting watching?'

Dangerous Liaison

Jaz was going hot and cold by turns. Her head ached and her nose ran, but it wasn't only a cold she was suffering from. Her stomach was tied in a million writhing knots. What to do? She couldn't think straight. All she wanted was to shake off these sinister characters she knew were sitting behind her on the bus for the Marina.

The bus driver was still waiting for the last few passengers to get on. A mum with a baby buggy and armfuls of shopping rushed towards the stop. Outside, the Volks Electric Railway trundled along the front, and shopkeepers of an optimistic nature displayed plastic shoes and sun cream. For a moment everything seemed to freeze. It had always been like this, and always would be, and Jaz was unable to move.

Then in an instant of crazy action she leapt off the bus, tripping over carrier bags and startling the baby into a high-pitched wail. Denim-Jacket and Grey-Mac jumped up behind her, but they were too late, as buggy and mother barred their way and the bus was moving off.

As it went uphill to the higher esplanade, Jaz darted across the road and zigzagged down into the Aquarium entrance. For a moment she thought it was a dead end, then she found the dark tunnel that led under the promenade to the beach. As she emerged from the subway no one seemed to be following.

On an impulse Jaz dashed up the steps back to the sea-front. On the Volks Railway platform, the bell rang for the departing train. People still queueing for tickets muttered their grumbles as Jaz pushed past. The train was just moving when Jaz jumped on.

It was hardly a high-speed getaway vehicle. It clattered on its narrow tracks at about bicycle pace, exactly as it had ever since Queen Victoria came to marvel at the wonders of electricity. It was open-sided and that made Jaz feel vulnerable.

'Excuse me.' She managed a brave stammer. 'Would you mind if I sat in the middle?' She pushed past some ample Crimplene-covered knees and squeezed herself between two ample nylon-covered bottoms.

'Angriphobia,' said the voice on her left. 'It's 'orrible, isn't it, ducks? My cousin Shirl 'ad it.'

The remark was addressed to Jaz so she made polite agreement.

'Couldn't go anywhere outside, our Shirl. Terrible it was, couldn't even sit on 'er balcony.'

'Nice balconies those flats 'ave,' commented the woman opposite, carefully taking a plastic rain-hood from her perm-tight curls.

As they continued to discuss Cousin Shirl's balcony, the woman on Jaz's right ventured some conversation.

'Not a nice day for it, eh love?'

'Er no,' Jaz agreed.

'Gets us out of the 'ouse, though. And we get a nice fish'n'chip lunch, and back in time for "Coronation Street". Can't complain.'

A bell rang and the train slowed. Jaz gulped with fear. Were they stopping? But it was only to shunt them on to a siding to let another train with a similar cargo of pensioners pass on the return trip.

'This brings back 'appy memories,' confided Jaz's neighbour. 'Came 'ere with Bert every year. We 'ad our 'oneymoon 'ere—only a couple of days, wartime, see—and then it was with the kids. 'Appy days.'

She sighed, then launched into a tremulous song: 'Oh I do like to be beside the seaside . . .' and all around Jaz the trippers took it up as they rode at a snail's pace ever nearer to the Marina.

'Airfield?'

Ted and Jo stared at each other in wordless alarm. Then Ted was fiddling with the radio and Jo was dashing downstairs and on to her bike.

She followed the path up-river, catching sight of Sebastian just as he crossed the main road. There the path continued and he took it, casual, hardly glancing round. The Customs men, wherever they were (and Jo, looking desperately round, couldn't see them) wouldn't be able to follow him here.

Cars hooted as a ginger-headed figure on a mountain bike hurtled across the road. Taking the path once more, Jo just glimpsed Sebastian before he was hidden behind sandy hillocks. She rode to the top of a hillock and halted, panting. Sebastian, still on the path, disappeared under the railway bridge. She freewheeled down the slope, bare and dusty from generations of BMX riders, and followed in Sebastian's tracks towards the airfield.

In the shadows of the railway bridge she paused. She had expected Sebastian to turn left, through the gate that led to the airfield, but he jogged steadily on. He was isolated now on the high narrow path, the river on his right, and on his left a deep water ditch, too wide to jump, and beyond it the high perimeter fence of the airfield.

Jo puzzled as a train rattled deafeningly overhead. She didn't think he could get into the airfield further up, but she couldn't be sure. There were two more bridges up ahead. First the old wooden toll bridge, only strong enough for pedestrians now, but leading back to the town; and beyond that the sweeping contours of the big bypass road bridge. Perhaps it was one of those that he was making for. Or there was always the river, lapping now right up to the banks. Who knew how many boats Sebastian had or where he kept them?

Or perhaps this was just a bit of healthy exercise, same as any day.

With a passport?

Doggedly she pedalled on.

The little train on the Promenade slowed to a halt. 'Brighton Marina!' called the driver. 'All change.'

Jaz waited politely for her companions to move. She was in no hurry to face what lay ahead.

'No, go on, ducks,' they told her. 'We're not getting out. There and back to see 'ow far it is, that's us.'

Jaz walked with leaden feet towards the Marina. Even if the Customs men weren't here to protect her, she decided, she had to go through with it. She still might discover some vital information.

She glanced nervously behind her. None of her followers were around. But didn't that woman look like the mumsy lady who sat behind her on the Shoreham bus? Couldn't be.

Just go on, don't look back. She remembered Sunday School stories about bands of angels being around people who walked into danger. 'I could do with some angels now, God,' she suggested as she passed through the archway into the Marina square.

All at once several things happened. A little man with oily hair and a face like a dachshund came and asked if she was Jasmine. 'Then plis would you like to come wid me.'

A rather larger man in dirty overalls loomed behind him, and Jaz realized she wasn't being offered a choice. They fell in each side of her and held her arms in a pincer-like grip, marching her out of the square towards the steel security gate, which provided the only way in to the rows of boats. There would have been no point in struggling.

Behind her there was some commotion. A taxi roared in and squealed to a halt. She turned to see the leather jackets leaping out. Blue-Denim and Grey-Mac came running, charging at the Leather-Jackets to cut them off as they raced towards her.

The little man was punching a code into a box by the gate. The gate clicked open and the larger of her captors put an unfriendly arm round her neck and pulled her through towards row upon row of neatly-moored boats. She could no longer see what was happening behind her, but she heard a clang as the gate locked automatically shut.

'Nothing to worry about, darlin',' he assured her. 'We don't want no more than what you've got to give us. It's just that the boss wants to see you.'

They took her down one of the long pontoons and stopped by a cruiser that would have been more at home in San Tropez than grey drizzly Sussex.

'Just to step aboard, plis,' said the oily man.

'No,' Jaz screamed. For the boat's engine was going, and a crewman stood, ropes in hand, ready to cast off. She tried to fumble for the envelope. 'Take it. I'm not coming.'

'Sorry darlin', but the boss wants a word.'

Then she did struggle. Tiredness, aches, pains and sniffles were forgotten as she fought to get free. She kicked and bit and screamed, but they lifted her like a featherweight. She was vaguely aware of feet running and voices yelling in the distance as they carried her down into the cabin and dumped her on to the cruiser's luxurious pile carpet.

She rolled over and looked up. A gentle pair of brown eyes were regarding her with amusement. An Asian face, Chinese maybe, looked at her thoughtfully.

'I'm so sorry for this inconvenience. Your friend Sebastian assures us you're just an innocent delivery service. In fact, he was at great pains to tell us. Not like him to care what happens to his carriers.'

The voices and footsteps got nearer. The engines revved and there was a clank of the gangway being hauled up.

'But for someone so innocent, you seem to have brought a lot of friends with you. So I'm afraid for the moment you must be our guest.'

There was a jolt as the boat started to move.

Wild-eyed, Jaz pulled herself up. No one tried to stop her. She turned towards the doorway.

She was facing the barrel of a gun.

Sebastian was still jogging. Jo was still following, pedalling like fury. He had almost reached the end of the airfield, the point at which planes waited before take-off. A small twin-engined plane stood there, propellers turning.

Sebastian slowed and glanced around. For a second his eyes met Jo's. Then he broke into a sprint, and Jo was pedalling for all she was worth. The gap between them had narrowed to school-hall length when he plunged off the high, raised path and down the bank to the left.

It was the airfield then. For a minute Jo paused and looked wildly around. How could she stop him on her own? On the distant road a car was parked. Two figures stood by it leaning on a wall. Frantically she waved at them, beckoning them towards her. If they were tourists they'd think she was mad, but they might just be the Investigations men. 'And if you are,' muttered Jo, 'Get over here—quick!'

Then she was pedalling again. She just had time to take in a narrow plank bridging the ditch and a gap in the fence beyond. 'Here goes,' she muttered and wished she still practised wheelies. The bike rose in the air as she went over the edge of the bank. It landed on the plank, and for moment she wobbled precariously over the deep muddy ditch. Somehow she steadied herself, made it across and headed for the gap.

Sebastian had slipped through easily but was it big enough for a bike? 'One way to find out,' muttered Jo and ducked. It was big enough—almost—but her sweatshirt caught on a wire and she fell, bike and all, wheels spinning on the ground. She was vaguely aware of blood and bruises as she picked up the bike and resumed the chase, following Sebastian in his last sprint for the waiting plane.

From the other side of the airfield two cars were racing. One plain blue, one white with familiar red and yellow markings. Police.

Sebastian was climbing on to the plane as Jo approached. Another figure was jumping out. Sebastian handed him a wad of bank notes and settled into the pilot's seat. 'Thanks Tony, you're a pal,' Jo heard him call as the aircraft began taxiing down the runway.

One cyclist and two cars converged at the point where the plane had just been. One cyclist, two Customs men and the luckless Tony (with a uniformed officer on either side) watched as the little plane lifted into the air, circled out over the sea and then turned back towards land. Jo stared hopelessly as it became nothing more than a black speck and disappeared over the Downs.

Jaz stood, swaying slightly, as the cruiser pulled out from the rows of moorings and into the outer harbour. The stone walls closed in as they neared the narrow exit to the open sea.

She could jump for it. A surprise somersault, knocking the man with the gun. Then a leap for the quayside. She looked around. There were four people in the cabin, three others on deck. The gun looked horribly real. This was no time for heroics. She didn't want to make the headlines as a tragedy.

The men on deck were shouting something she couldn't hear. 'Get back,' said the man with the gun. 'Sit down.' But her legs wouldn't move. Fear paralyzed every bit of her body. Her head was swimming. The engines gave a sudden deafening rush of noise and the man raised the gun.

There was a terrible cracking noise and she was falling. Then everything went black.

25

Drops in the Ocean

Jaz got her newspaper headline, although she never went past the newsagent's to see it.

Deep into the night the papers rolled off the presses.

DRUGS BARON CAUGHT IN BRIGHTON RAID
Customs officials yesterday announced one of the biggest ever breakthroughs in their battle against drug smuggling. James Tan, boss of an international criminal network which ran from Bangkok to Brighton, was arrested on his luxury yacht whilst making a dramatic getaway attempt from Brighton Marina.

A Customs cutter and several smaller launches were used to block the harbour entrance and prevent Tan's escape. Eye-witness Kevin Slater was fishing on the harbour wall at the time of the incident: 'All of a sudden some boats came from nowhere and lined up across the harbour entrance. Then I saw a big posh cruiser making straight for the blockade. It was going at a fair old lick, so I shouted a warning. It didn't slow down, just carried on and rammed one of the boats head on.'

Tan's ramming attempt almost succeeded in pushing through the blockade, but Customs officials leapt on board the vessel and made the arrest. Witnesses report that they heard shots being fired as the vessel was boarded.

There are unconfirmed reports that Tan had taken a hostage, a teenage girl acting as a courier . . .

Jaz was woken first by the snoring. Then there were the groans, the footsteps and the rattling of metal trolleys. In the eerie twilight she saw a body being wheeled past.

'If I am dead,' she thought, 'this certainly isn't heaven.'

The night sister noticed Jaz's stirrings and came over.

'Hello, our heroine's awake. How are you feeling?'

Jaz thought for a moment. 'My head hurts . . . What am I . . .? Oh, I know, I got shot.'

'Shot? No, my dear, concussion, that's all. You fainted. Fell and cracked your head on a table. They kept you in for observation, but you'll be right as rain in the morning. Now why don't you go back to sleep?'

Jaz needed no persuading. But Ward 2E was not the best place for sleep. She drifted in and out of confused dreams, where Chinese men in pyjamas snored on thick pile carpets, nurses rode on electric trains that sailed out to sea, and the woman in the next bed smiled at her just like the mumsy lady on the bus.

. . . Customs were first alerted to the smuggling operation when a holiday yachtsman noticed a lone boatman hauling something up from the sea bed by

*night. The canister was later recovered and found to
contain heroin with a street value of more than one and
a half million pounds.*

*'It's a good day for British law enforcement,' said
Customs officer Tim Jefferson, who masterminded the
raid, codenamed 'Operation Whiteflower'. 'Customs
will continue to be vigilant in preventing the evil of
drugs from reaching our shores. The public can be a
great help to us by reporting anything suspicious. We
would like to commend the yachtsman, Edward Carter,
for his public-spirited action'* . . .

'Yeah. Well done, Ted,' said Jo bitterly. 'And we
don't even get a mention.'

She put the newspaper down in disgust.

'Think yourself lucky,' said Ted, spooning sugar into
his tea. 'The press have been camped round my
doorstep since five o'clock this morning. If I hadn't
slipped out the back way, and come down here, I'd be a
prisoner in my own home.'

'That's OK,' said Maggie Thomas. 'Stay as long as
you like.'

'Thanks.' She and Ted exchanged glances that Jo
thought bordered dangerously on the sloppy.

'Yeah well, you two enjoy yourselves. I'm going to
see Jaz.'

'Are you sure she's up to visitors?'

'She'd better be. I wanna tell her off for getting all
the best adventures.'

Jaz opened her eyes and it was daylight. She shut
them. An image was printed on her eyelids—people
by the bed: Mum and Dad and Jo clutching a

245

newspaper. She opened her eyes again.

'Did they get Sebastian?' was her first question.

'No,' said Jo flatly. 'He flew off.' She described the getaway without excitement. 'Can you believe it? After all that . . .'

She brightened. 'Never mind, you done good.' She chucked Jaz the newspaper. 'You got the worst villain of all—even though Mr bloomin' Customs Jefferson thinks he did it all himself.'

Jaz read the article, slowly, as the Walcotts kept asking how she was feeling and the nurse came to take her temperature. She ran her finger down as she read. The newsprint seemed to dance in front of her eyes this morning.

> . . . *Two armed men, said to be of a rival gang to Tan's, were also captured at the Marina. They are being held pending police enquiries.*
>
> *Later reports confirm two Customs officials are in hospital recovering from bullet wounds. They are both said to be in a stable condition. Also injured was Customs official Maria Browning, who attempted to board the vessel as it left its moorings. Her condition is described as 'not serious' . . .*

In a far corner of the ward, the TV flickered relentlessly. They caught the distant beat of a stirring signature tune. 'Lunchtime news,' said Mrs Walcott. 'Ssh, let's see if there's anything on.'

Jo darted across the ward and turned up the sound. It was the usual boring stuff until . . .

'The dramatic capture yesterday of drugs baron James Tan has led to a wave of further arrests.

Susanna Bligh brings us this report . . .'

An earnest young woman perched in front of rows of pontoon-parked yachts was talking to camera.

'James Tan, aged twenty-eight, was born in Singapore and educated at a British public school. It was not the money, he said, but the adventure, which drew him to the international drugs trade. From his luxury yacht he ran a chain which stretched from the poppy fields of Thailand to the inner-city estates of Britain, and his capture is hailed as a major breakthrough in the fight against trafficking.'

Cut to a man speaking against flashing cameras and a crush of journalists.

'That's our Customs man,' said Jaz.

'Customs Investigator Tim Jefferson,' said the caption.

'Although the actual haul of heroin which led to his arrest is a drop in the ocean compared to the vast amount coming into the country each year, the significance of this operation is that we have rounded up most of the key players in a huge ring.'

Cut to some grainy photos.

'Maxim Gorodski, a strip-bar owner from North London, was one of four drug dealers also arrested yesterday. The owner and captain of a cargo ship operating out of Dieppe were also taken into custody by French authorities. Raymond Smith, twenty-six, a friend of Tan's from public school days and thought to be in charge of Tan's activities within Britain, was captured yesterday afternoon in Redhill, Surrey . . .'

Jaz sat up in bed. 'But they did get him! Sebastian— they did get him!'

Jo looked blankly at her.

'Raymond Smith! That's him, that's his real name. They got him!' Jo peered at the blurred photo on the screen. Dark hair and glasses, but unmistakably Sebastian.

'They got 'im!' she yelled. Several faces glared at her from across the ward. An elderly man in a neck brace climbed out of bed and turned off the TV.

'Redhill—wonder what he was doing there,' said Jaz.

'I could explain that.' The voice, coming from behind the curtains round the next bed, made them all jump.

A nurse pulled back the curtain and the mumsy lady from the bus gave them a big smile.

So it wasn't a dream, thought Jaz, or am I even more confused than I thought I was?

'He flew to an airfield near Redhill,' continued the woman, 'and got a taxi into the town. They caught him in a men's outfitters, buying some clothes. He was heading for Gatwick to catch a scheduled flight. He'll never get it now.'

Jo and Jaz looked dumbfounded at the stranger's knowledge. The woman smiled again. 'Maria Browning, HM Customs and Excise. And you led us quite a dance, Miss Walcott.'

'You! I thought it was the men in leather jackets.'

'Yes, they were following you all right, but not for your safety. That envelope you were carrying had a key in it—the key to a suitcase in a left-luggage locker at Kings Cross. Inside was forty thousand pounds in used notes, and those jokers knew that. They knew because they were the dealers who paid it to Smith in the first place. They knew he had to get it to Tan, so they thought it would be a good trick to reclaim it before it got there.'

'So the scruffy bloke in denim, and the shifty one in the grey mac—I got that all wrong. They were nothing to do with it?'

The woman smiled again. 'Mark Simms and Gary Morrison did have quite a lot to do with it. They wouldn't just send me on my own. Although it was only me who kept up with you on the train. I was just behind when Tan's boys got you. Unfortunately, they got me too. And they weren't so gentle with me.'

'Why? What did they do?' asked Jo.

'Jodi, don't be so nosy,' said Mrs Walcott.

'It's no secret,' said the detective, 'and it could have been worse. A few broken ribs, rather a lot of bruises—nothing that won't mend. But to be honest, Miss Walcott, we were amazed it didn't happen to you.

'But then we read Smith's—Sebastian's—note. He said he was leaving the business. He said he wouldn't grass on Tan on one condition: "Don't shoot the messenger," that's how he put it. "If you harm her, I'll harm you. The girl's innocent." Then he wrote something quite strange. He said: "That's something you and I missed out on—innocence. Probably too late to find it now, but I've got a crazy urge to try. I'm getting out. I've had enough".'

There was a silence.

'So he wasn't all bad,' remarked Jo.

'Very few people are,' said the Customs officer. 'If they were, our job would be simple.' She nursed her aching ribs. 'Although I suppose it might be even more dangerous.'

'Look, it's simple. When I shout "sheet", you just pull this rope over here.'

'Ted, I don't see why you need to shout at all. Sailing's supposed to be calm and restful.'

'And so it will be, Maggie, if you just do what you're told.'

The wind caught *Mary Jane*'s sails and Maggie's answer was lost in the breeze.

'He won't get far with my mum, if he expects her to do what she's told,' said Jo to Jaz, as they stood watching *Mary Jane*'s latest crew member.

Jo skimmed pebbles out over the waves. 'Come on, Gary, you try.' Gary's stone plopped into the sea. 'Nah, try a flat one, like this.'

It was autumn half-term and an unexpectedly warm day had tempted Ted into one last sail before winter, and the Walcotts out to watch. Gary was home for the week, with a note from the school saying how delighted they were with his progress.

'He's learnt to fold his pyjamas and say thank you when people pass him things,' said Jo with pride.

'That's progress?' asked Alex, who was searching for crabs.

'Course it is, for him.'

'Might be progress for you too, if you picked your clothes off the bedroom floor,' said the Rev.

'Well, thank you, Dad. Thank you for your most excellent advice.'

Gary, for whom taking advice was no simple matter, continued to chuck pebbles awkwardly into the sea. Pastor Walcott came and put his hand over Gary's, gently turning it to the right angle. The next pebble plopped just the same. They kept trying.

Jaz was up on the breakwater, balancing gracefully on its slippery top. Suddenly she did a perfect somersault and landed without a wobble.

'Has the girl no fear?' asked the Rev. 'Jasmine, come down and stop showing off. We all know how brave you are.'

This last remark referred to a letter the Customs people had written commending Jasmine Walcott for bravery.

'This isn't brave,' she explained, 'because I'm not scared. I've practised it and practised it and I know I can do it. You can only be brave if really you're scared, otherwise it isn't bravery.'

She flipped over again.

'You know,' said Pastor Walcott to Jo, 'I'm sorry you didn't get a letter. You're a plucky character, if ever I met one.'

'Me?' For a moment Jo was lost for words. She stared at the sea. 'Well, who needs a rotten old letter? God sees. You told me that.'

Pastor Walcott looked mystified. 'I did?'

'He did?' Jaz thought, overhearing from her perch.

'Yeah, you know, the voice in the lav,' explained Jo, suddenly embarrassed.

'Oh, that old story.' Jaz had heard it loads of times before.

'D'you reckon he really does?' asked Jo. 'God, I mean. Does he see everything?'

'Yes,' said Pastor Walcott. 'I reckon.'

Funny, pondered Jaz, balancing steadily with one leg

outstretched, you can hear things so often you forget they're true. There's someone sees me quite different from anyone else—not just my skin colour, my gym prizes, my stupid shyness. It was a comforting thought.

'Bit scarey,' said Jo suddenly.

Mmm, thought Jaz, that too.

A crunch of pebbles drew her attention to the other side of the breakwater. A young man carrying a sailboard was picking his way down the beach.

'Hey,' she hissed to Jo. 'Getta load of that.'

Jo climbed up to see. The young man was zipping up his wet suit over a broad muscled torso, and his dark wavy hair was blowing in the breeze. He looked up and his brown eyes caught them staring. 'Hi girls.'

Jaz and Jo giggled as he ran down to the sea.

'Now he's what I call a hunk,' said Jaz.

'Mmm,' agreed Jo. 'I could fancy him.'

Up on the breakwater they breathed the salt air and surveyed their world. On one side the windsurfer fixed his sail with deft movements. On the other Gary threw clumsily, his face contorted with the effort. Out at sea, Ted barked fierce orders—but Maggie's answer was teasing and he relaxed into a smile.

Then Jo laughed. 'You'd think we'd learn.'

'What?'

'Well, you know, appearances are only skin deep.'

Pastor Walcott guided Gary's throwing once more. They watched them, black hand over white one, try and try again. At last a perfect flattened pebble and a moment of smooth calm sea. The stone bounced, not once or twice, but four times. Gary laughed, a daft infectious chortle, that had them all laughing with him as the tide went sucking out and the ripples died away.

Also from Lion Publishing:

In Deep Water

Veronica Heley

'You'll be scared of water for the rest of your life,'
Nicola told Jan, 'if you don't do something about it.'

A boating accident has left Jan terrified of water,
reluctant to face up to her fear. But when Nicola takes
up synchro-swimming Jan allows herself to be talked
round—provided her friend will be around to
encourage and help.

When Nicola finds a more compelling interest—
good-looking Kerry—Jan is devastated. There's the
swimming gala coming up, so she has to stay in the
synchro team, but she knows she can't cope at the pool
on her own. Until Clemmie comes to the rescue.

ISBN 0 7459 2399 2

Relative Danger

Janice Brown

'Jon, it's only your father, not King Kong. Why do
you...?'

'Look, you don't know him. I don't know him either,
come to that. But you wouldn't like him, I guarantee it.
Even *you* couldn't find something nice to say about
him.'

On holiday with his long-estranged and moody
father, Jon quickly finds they have little in common
and even less to talk about. Boredom sets in. Then he
sees Casey.

She seems just his kind of girl—but what is she
really like? How can he get to know her? Jon's chance
comes when a strange and chilling chain of events
unexpectedly throws the two together.

ISBN 0 7459 2539 1